Hotel Savoy

Published by Hesperus Press Limited
28 Mortimer Street, London W1W 7RD
www.hesperuspress.com

This translation first published by Hesperus Press Limited, 2013
© Joseph Roth, 1924

English translation and introduction © Jonathan Katz, 2013

Designed and typeset by Fraser Muggeridge studio

Printed in Great Britain by CPI Group (UK) Ltd, Croydon, CR0 4YY

ISBN: 978-1-84391-386-3

Hotel Savoy

Joseph Roth

Translated from the German by Jonathan Katz

Introduction

(New readers are advised that this Introduction discusses elements of the plot.)

One of the finest German language authors of the first half of the twentieth century, Joseph Roth was born to Jewish parents on 2 September 1894 in Brody, then little more than a *shtetl* in East Galicia, at that time a territory of the Habsburg Austro-Hungarian Empire, and now in Ukraine. He began his higher education in nearby Lemberg (now Lviv) and in 1914 moved to the University in Vienna to study literature. He served in the Imperial Army on the Eastern Front in 1916, not as a combatant but as a writer and military reporter. After demobilisation and eventual return to Vienna in 1918 – an experience which must to some extent have informed his compassionate depiction of the *Heimkehrer* (returning soldiers, or 'homecomers') in *Hotel Savoy* – he wrote for leftist newspapers there until moving to Berlin in 1920, when he started writing for the more prominent liberal press, an early career in which he was soon employed by important papers in Frankfurt and Prague.

The rest of Roth's story, of a life which brought him literary distinction through both journalism and a series of first-rate novels (the best known among them being the great family and historical saga *The Radetzky March*), but ended in Paris in 1939 in tragic exile, isolation and personal despair, has been told often enough to engender both familiarity and puzzlement. For it easy to view his political convictions as an uneasy, unsteady course of false starts, involving some considerable wishful thinking, dissemblance and self-deception; this view has also conditioned the reading of his work, in which, between those early apparently socialist leanings of the 1920s and later flirtations with Catholicism and monarchist revivalism, we may see him turning from one end of the political spectrum to the other. Furthermore – and here is a critical phenomenon by no means unique to Joseph Roth – the brilliantly accomplished later work has sometimes been seen as a creative culmination, towards which the early writing is more tentatively feeling its way, with occasional bright flashes revealing what was to come.

Taken on their own terms, however, in the context of what preceded rather than what followed, the early works seem to show a much less defined political position, and a more ironic overview, of all that presented itself to the author in the immediate post-war society he examines. Roth's first two novels, *The Spider's Web* and *Hotel Savoy*, portray in powerfully stark terms the condition of human nature under the immense pressure of turbulent economic and political uncertainty.

The Spider's Web was first published in a newspaper serial form in 1923. The writing is already highly accomplished, owing no doubt much to Roth's experience and preoccupations with both political and more 'occasional' (*feuilletons*) journalism. *Hotel Savoy* was also first published in the Frankfurt newspaper in 1924, but was then in the same year issued as a volume by a reputable literary publisher, and was considered by Roth himself to be his first real novel. To the psychological depth and the storyteller's skill of the first work, *Hotel Savoy* adds the formal ploy of a first-person narrator, and the emotional intensity and epigrammatic economy of a lyric poet.

The main character of *The Spider's Web*, Theodor Lohse, is an ex-lieutenant from the First World War who has taken up law studies and is struggling both with external circumstances and with his own personal insecurities and mediocre talents to establish himself in a new career. Manipulated by forces more powerful, and by persons more talented, than himself, his 'progress' and decline make him something of a sample case of recruitment to fascism, poisonous anti-Semitism and eventual moral worthlessness. *Hotel Savoy* takes us still a little further back in the post-war story, when the homecoming demobilised soldiers are still flooding out from the east to form an ominous undercurrent of unrest, a prelude to the upheavals to come.

Already as a journalist Roth had made it his business not only to report but to extrapolate, speculate, predict. Such combined insights are creatively deployed both in the narrative plot and setting of the novel, and in its curiously ambivalent first-person observer. This narrator, Gabriel Dan, is himself a returner. After long internment as a prisoner of war in Siberia he has endured a grueling journey out of captivity towards a new life in the 'West', a future in which he seems by his own admission to have little firm belief. In reality he feels himself to be more permanently on the move, happy just to be 'stripping away an old life once again'. Arriving at a border town placed physically and symbolically between East and West – Roth never names the place but it is almost certainly intended to be the town of Łódź – where he knows he has relatives he hopes might be able to help him, he puts up at the monumental Hotel Savoy, at once a vividly drawn microcosm, containing the full spectrum of life's luxuries and degradations, and an evocative symbol of the political and moral state of a society now in the control of dark and threatening forces. The hotel's residents fall 'victim' to it, and those with the weaker defences eventu-ally perish violently along with it.

Ambivalent certainly, but also self-knowing and self-critical, Dan is in a way saved by his own detachment and noninvolve-ment. Or rather, he is narrowly saved from death, but he is also condemned to witness the departure of those whose lives he seems to admire as more authentic and vital than his own. His splendidly independent-minded friend Zwonimir Pansin, the wild proto-revolutionary, engages Dan's affection and understanding with his outraged observations of inequality, unfairness and the exploitation of one class by another; but there is also an obtuse-ness and a perverseness in Zwonimir, a self-absorbed recklessness that prevents him from genuinely appreciating, let alone serving, his own interests or the common good.

Gabriel Dan, ruefully recollecting that even in the war he was able to think only of his own life and his own death ('I walked over corpses, and sometimes it troubled me that I felt no pain') is ultimately forced to confront himself too, as the impassive individualist he is, a 'cold creature' who has 'nothing in common with any crowd'; and as such he is powerless to rescue or redeem even the more attractive of the hotel's other resident victims – the loveable clown Santschin, or the girl Dan wishes to love but cannot bring himself even to address honestly and committedly, and whom in the end he chooses, despite some self-recrimination, to abandon, while deceiving himself that the failure is partly hers.

For some readers the most poignant relationship of all will be the affection Dan unexpectedly discovers with that very different 'homecomer', their former fellow townsman now turned American millionaire. Bloomfield's arrival from America, awaited with such fervent longing by the townspeople who delude themselves that he is coming as a saviour to banish all their miseries, has in reality a very different reason for returning, and becomes the unwitting cause of their further lapse into inertia and hopelessness. But there are those few who do know, and have known all along, what brings Bloomfield home, and to them, and through them to Gabriel Dan, he is able to impart something more lasting.

Amidst the pathos, and amidst the hotel's grotesque world of rascals and inadequates and lame ducks and shysters, there are moments of comedy and burlesque, and moments of tenderness, through which Gabriel passes as the ever neutral, ironic observer. The eventual violent destruction of that world, and the hints of a more general and spreading conflagration beyond it, leave him, and us, finally travelling on, on a slow train, towards some indeterminate future.

– *Jonathan Katz, May 2013*

Book One

I

I arrive at ten o'clock in the morning at the Hotel Savoy. I have decided to rest for a few days or a week. This is the town where my relatives live – my parents were Russian Jews. I want to get some money together and continue my journey to the West.

I am returning after three years as a prisoner of war; I was in a Siberian prison camp, and I've wandered through Russian villages and towns as a worker, day-labourer, night watchman, porter, baker's assistant.

I am wearing a Russian smock someone gave me, short breeches I got from a comrade who died, and boots, still serviceable – now I can't even remember myself where they came from.

For the first time in five years I am standing once again at the gates of Europe. It looks to me – this Hotel Savoy – more European than any other Eastern Hotel, with its seven floors and its gilded coat of arms and liveried porter. It promises water, soap, English-style toilet, a lift, maids in white caps, chamber pots with a friendly gleam to them like priceless surprise gifts in little brown-inlaid cabinets; there'll be electric lamps, with the light blossoming from pink and green shades like flowers from the calyx, and bells ringing out brightly at the press of a button, and real beds with eiderdown quilts billowing, cheerfully ready to welcome the body.

I am happy to be stripping away an old life once again, as so often over these years. I see in my mind the soldier, the murderer, the man almost murdered, the man resurrected, the captive in chains, the wanderer.

I sense early-morning haze, hear the drum-roll of troops on the march rattling the window-panes at the tops of the buildings, I see a man in white shirt-sleeves, and the jerking arms of the soldiers, and a glow in the woods, the gleam of the morning dew; I plunge into the grass before my 'imaginary foe' and feel that burning desire to stay there, for always, right there in the velvet grass that strokes my face.

I hear the silence of the sick-bay, the white silence. I rise from my bed on a summer's morning, hear the trilling of lively larks, enjoy the taste of morning cocoa with buttered rolls and the odour of iodine in the day's 'first diet'.

I am living in a white world made of sky and snow, the ground covered in a sallow mange of barrack buildings. I take in one last sweet drag on a foraged cigarette butt; I read the advertisements page of an ancient newspaper from my home town, from which I can recall the familiar street-names, and recognise the man running the local grocery store, and a porter, and one blond Agnes whom I once slept with.

I hear the blissful sound of rain in a sleepless night, and the icicles rapidly melting under the smiling morning sun, and I clasp the ample breasts of a woman I met along my way and lay with on the moss, the white splendour of her thighs. I sleep the profoundest sleep amid the hay, in the barn. I stride over furrowed fields, and drink in the frail singing of a balalaika.

You can absorb so much, and yet remain unchanged in body, and in gait and manner, you can quaff from any number of vessels and never have your fill, just as a rainbow may glitter in all its colours but still in the end remain a rainbow with just the same palette.

I could turn up here at the Hotel Savoy with one shirt, and leave as the proud owner of twenty trunks – and I'd still be the same Gabriel Dan. Perhaps it is realising this that has made me so self-assured, so proud and grandiose that the porter salutes me, me the mere vagrant in a Russian smock, and a servant boy dances attendance even though I have no luggage.

I am taken up by a lift, mirrors adorning every side of it; the lift-boy, a man already advanced in years, lets the rope slip through his hands, the compartment rises, and I sway with it – I think to myself, I could so easily fly aloft like this for a good

4

long time. I love this swaying, and reckon how many wearying steps I'd have to clamber up if I weren't able to sit in this splendid lift; and I hurl back down all my bitterness, and my hardship and wandering and homelessness, my beggar's life now in the past – I hurl it all deep down, from where it can never reach me again as I soar up and up on high.

My room – I have been given one of the cheapest – is up on the sixth floor and bears the number 703. That appeals to me – I am superstitious about numbers; the nought in the middle is like a lady with an older and a younger gentleman on either side. On the bed there is a yellow coverlet, thank God not a grey one to remind me of army service. I switch the light on and off a few times, I open up the bedside cabinet, the mattress gives under my hand and springs up again, water glistens from a carafe, the window looks out onto back yards, where gaily coloured laundry flutters and children shout and hens strut around freely.

I wash, and slide slowly into bed, savouring every moment. I open the window, the hens are clucking loudly and cheerfully; it is like a sweet lullaby. I sleep a dreamless sleep, the whole day long.

II

Late sunshine was reddening the topmost windows of the house opposite; the laundry and hens and children and had disappeared from the yard.

In the morning, when I arrived, there had been light rain. In the meantime it had become bright again, and I felt as if I'd slept not one but three days. My tiredness was gone; I was in fine spirits. I was curious about the town, and this new life of mine. My room felt friendly, as if I'd already lived there for a long time, and the bell was now familiar, and the push-button, and the electric switch, the green lampshade, wardrobe and washbasin. Everything homely, as in a room where you've spent your childhood, everything making for calm and comfort and warmth, as it is when you have been reunited with someone you love. Only one thing was new: a notice pinned to the door, with the words:

'After 10.00 pm quiet is kindly requested. No liability accepted for missing valuables. Safe deposit in hotel. Respectfully, Kalegyropoulos, Proprietor.'

It was a foreign name, Greek. I had a little fun declining it: Kalegyropoulos, Kalegyropoulou, Kalegyropoul – a hazy memory of cheerless school lessons; a Greek teacher surfacing again from a forgotten era, in his patina-green jacket. I decided to walk around the town, perhaps go and find a relative if there was enough time, and enjoy myself, if enjoyment was on offer this evening in this place. I went along the corridor to the main staircase, relishing the fine stone slabs of the hotel passageway, the red stonework, and the echo of my firm footsteps.

I went slowly down the stairs. Voices were coming from the floors below; up here it was all quiet, all the doors were closed, and it was as if you were in an old monastery and walking past the cells of monks at prayer. The fifth floor looked exactly like the sixth; you could easily mistake one for the other. Both there and down here there were hotel clocks on the wall overlooking the staircase, only the two were not showing the same time. It was ten past seven on the sixth floor, and here just seven o'clock. Then on the fourth floor it was another ten minutes earlier.

Over the flagstones on the third floor there are dark red carpets with green borders, and you can't hear your footsteps any more. The room numbers aren't painted on the doors here, but set on little oval porcelain plaques. A girl comes along with a feather duster and a wastepaper basket; there is apparently more attention paid to cleanliness down here. This is where the rich live; Kalegyropoulos, cunning fellow, deliberately keeps the clocks slow, because rich people have plenty of time. On the raised ground floor the two leaves of a door stood wide open.

It was a large room with two windows, two beds, two chests of drawers, a green plush sofa, a brown tile stove and a stand for luggage. There was no copy of Kalegyropoulos's notice to be seen on the door – perhaps the residents on the upper ground floor were permitted to make a noise after ten o'clock, and perhaps liability was accepted for these people's 'missing valuables' – or were they already aware of the hotel safe deposit, or did Kalegyropoulos perhaps tell them in person?

A woman came rustling out of a neighbouring room, perfumed and in a grey feather boa. There's a real lady! I said to myself, and followed closely after her down the few steps, looking in admiration at her little patent-leather boots. She paused for a short while at the porter's lodge. I got to the door at the same time as she did; the porter saluted, and I was flattered to think that maybe he took me for the rich lady's companion.

Not knowing any of the directions here, I decided to follow along behind the lady.

She turned right out of the narrow lane where the hotel stood, from where the marketplace broadened out. It must have been market day, hay and straw lying scattered on the paving, people just now shutting up the shops, locks clinking, chains rattling, pedlars making their way home with their little hand-carts, women in gaily coloured head-scarves hurrying along and carefully holding brimming pots in front of them, overflowing bags on their arms, with wooden kitchen spoons poking out. The occasional street lantern threw a silvery glow into the twilight; the pavements were turning into a Corso, with men in uniform and in civilian clothes sporting slim canes, and there were intermittent wafts of sweet Russian scent. Carriages came jolting along from the station, with luggage piled high and passengers all muffled up. The road was rough, full of potholes and sudden dips; over some of the damaged places there were rotten wooden boards that rattled disconcertingly.

And yet the town looked more friendly in the evening than during the day. In the morning it had been grey, coal dust from nearby factories billowing out over it from giant chimneys, grimy beggars grovelled on the street corners, rubbish and slop buckets lay piled up in narrow side streets. But now all of this, all the filth and ordure, poverty and pestilence, all was hidden in the darkness – kindly, motherly darkness, forgiving, concealing.

Houses, frail and dilapidated, appear ghostly, mysterious in the dark, arbitrary in their architecture. Crooked gables are softened in the shadows, meagre light confidentially lures and beckons through half-darkened windows, and then just two steps later there is light streaming out from a confectionery shop, through windows tall as a man, mirrors reflecting the glare of crystal and chandeliers, angels charmingly hovering and swooping from the ceiling. This is the confectionery shop of the rich man's world, with money to earn and money to spend in this industrial town.

This was where the lady went, but I didn't follow her in; I reflected that my money would have to last some time yet before I could travel further.

I strolled on, saw little black clusters of quick-witted kaftan-clad Jews, overheard loud mutterings, greetings and counter-greetings, angry retorts, lengthy discourse; talk of feathers, percentages, hops, steel, coal, lemons, went flying round, discharged into the air by mouths, aimed at ears. Suspicious-looking men with rubber collars – apparently policemen. I reached automatically for my breast pocket, where I had my passport, just as I always used to reach for my cap when I was in the army and someone in authority was around. I was a soldier coming home, my papers were in order, I had nothing to fear.

I went up to a policeman and asked how to get to Gibka, which was where my relatives were living, my rich uncle Phoebus Böhlaug. The policeman spoke German. Lots of people spoke German here; in this town German manufacturers, engineers and tradesmen predominated in society, business and industry.

It took ten minutes to walk there, during which I thought about Phoebus Böhlaug. Back home in the Leopoldstadt my father had spoken of him with envy and hatred, after coming back tired and dejected from fruitless council meetings. The name Phoebus had always been spoken with respect by every member of the family, as if they really were speaking of the Sun God himself. It was only my father who habitually referred to him as 'Phoebus, the lout' – because allegedly he had been up to something suspicious with my mother's dowry. My father had always been too much of a coward, and had never demanded the dowry; he'd never gone further than scanning the guest list to see if Phoebus Böhlaug had checked in at the Hotel Imperial, and if he was indeed there my father would go and invite his brother-in-law for tea in the Leopoldstadt. My mother used to wear black, along with what had become rather sparse finery, and she respected her rich brother as if he were something exotic, or royal, and they hadn't been borne of the same womb or suckled by the same breasts. My uncle would arrive bearing a book for me, and there'd be a smell of gingerbread from the dark kitchen where my grandfather lived without ever emerging except on festive occasions, when he came forth like some new creation, freshly washed, wearing a white starched shirt-front, eyes twinkling through glasses that were far too weak, bending forward to take a look at his son Phoebus, the pride of his old age. Phoebus had a broad laugh, not to mention his considerable double chin and rolling red neck fat; he reeked of cigars, and sometimes of wine, and he kissed everybody on both cheeks. He talked a great deal, loudly and merrily, but you only had to ask him whether business was going well and his eyes would bulge out and he'd collapse in on himself, and you'd think any moment he'd start shivering like some beggar perishing in the cold, his double chin disappearing under his collar: 'Business? The way things are now, it's finished! When I was a young lad you could get a seed-cake for half a kopek; now it's ten kopeks for a loaf of bread! The children – touch wood – they're growing up, and that costs something too; Alexander's asking for pocket money every day of the week!'

My father would fiddle with his jacket cuffs and then rest his hands back on the edge of the table; he smiled when Phoebus spoke to him, but it was a weak, cryptic smile, really willing a heart attack on his brother-in-law. After two hours Phoebus would stand up, press a silver coin into my mother's hand, then another for my grandfather, and finally a nice big shiny one into my pocket. As it was dark my father accompanied him down the steps, holding the paraffin lamp high up in his hand, and Mother would call, 'Nathan, be careful of the shade!' Father was careful of the shade, and as the door was open you could still hear old Phoebus chatting away lustily.

Two days later Phoebus was off on his travels, and Father would announce: 'The lout's off again.'

'That's enough of that, Nathan!' Mother would say.

I arrived at the Gibka. This is a smart street in the suburbs with white, low-built houses, new and ornamental. I saw the windows were lit up in the Böhlaugs' house, but the door was closed. I considered for a while whether I ought to go up there this late in the evening – it must have been ten by now – and then I heard a piano playing, and a cello, a woman's voice, and the clatter of playing cards. I thought it was quite out of the question to arrive in that company dressed in the kind of suit I was wearing. My first appearance meant everything; I decided to postpone my visit till the next day, and made my way back to the hotel.

After my fruitless journey I was feeling disgruntled. The porter didn't greet me this time when I entered. The lift-man was clearly in no hurry when I pressed the bell; he took his time coming over, looked me enquiringly in the face. He was a man around fifty, in uniform, distinctly ageing for a lift-boy. It annoyed me that in this hotel they didn't have rosy-cheeked young lads operating the lift.

I remembered then that I'd still wanted to have a look at the seventh floor, and I took the stairs. The corridor up there was very narrow, the roof lower, and there was a grey mist emanating from a laundry room, and a smell of wet washing. There must have been two or three doors half open; you could hear people arguing. There was, as I had rightly guessed, no clock up here. I was just about to go down the stairs again when the lift grated to a halt, the gate opened, the lift-man gave me a surprised glance, and let out a young girl wearing a small grey sports hat. As she turned towards me I saw her face was brown, her eyes large and grey with black lashes. I wished her good evening, and went downstairs. Something made me look back up again from the last step, and I thought I caught those beer-tinted eyes of the ageing lift-boy glancing down at me over the banister.

I locked my door, feeling some indefinable fear, and began reading an old book.

III

I was not sleepy. The bell of a church tower entrusts its regular strokes to the tender night. Above me I can hear footsteps, gentle, soft, unceasing steps, surely a woman's – was it the young girl up in the seventh floor walking up and down so restlessly? What was the matter with her?

I looked up at the ceiling; I had a sudden feeling it had become transparent. Perhaps the graceful soles of the girl in grey might come into view. Was she walking around barefoot, or in slippers? Or in grey stockings of half-silk?

I remembered how yearningly I and many comrades of mine had waited for our leave, when we'd be able to relieve our longing for a pair of low buckskin shoes. We'd find healthy peasant-girls' legs for stroking – those broad feet, the big toe standing a little apart, which would have walked through the mud in the fields and trodden the sludge of the country road, and bodies, for which the hardened soil of a frozen autumn field served as a love-bed. Sturdy thighs. A fleeting moment of love in the dark, before the order came to interrupt us. I thought of that already ageing schoolteacher in the military zone, the only woman in the place not to have fled from war and invasion. She was a sharp creature, over thirty, they called her the 'barbed wire mesh'. But show me the man who wouldn't have wooed her; for miles around she was the only woman with proper shoes and stockings – for all the holes in them.

In this huge Hotel Savoy, in all of its eight hundred and sixty-four rooms, and in fact throughout this whole town, there were perhaps only two people awake, I myself and the young girl up above me. We could very well be lying next to each other, I, Gabriel, and a brown young girl with a friendly face and those large grey eyes with their black eyelashes. How thin the ceilings must be here, for those gazelle-like steps to be heard so clearly. I fancied I could even catch the scent of her body. I decided to go and see if the footsteps really were hers.

In the corridor there was a dark red glow from a small lamp. Shoes, boots, women's low shoes, stood outside the doors of the rooms, all of them wearing expressions just like human faces. On the seventh floor there was no lamp burning anywhere, just dim light coming through frosted glass panes. A thin yellow beam shone through a crack – it was room 800 – this must be the restless walker's room. I can see through the keyhole – yes, it is the girl. She is pacing up and down in a white gown – a bathrobe – and now she stops for a while at the table, looks at a book, and starts walking once again.

I try hard to catch a glimpse of her face – but all I see is the delicate curve of her chin, a quarter of her profile when she stands still, a bunch of hair, and, when she takes a larger step and the folds of her robe rise up, a gleam of brown skin. A laboured cough came from somewhere, and someone spat noisily into a vessel. I went back to my own room. As I was closing the door I thought I saw a shadow in the corridor; I pulled the door wide open again so that the light from my room lit up a part of the hallway. But there had been no one there.

Up above me the footsteps stopped. The girl was probably asleep now. I lay down on the bed fully clothed and pulled back the curtains from the window. The soft grey of first daylight spread gently over the contents of the room.

Morning's inexorable approach was announced by the sharp ring of a doorbell and the brutish shout of a man's voice in some incomprehensible language.

A room waiter came – he was wearing a green cobbler's apron, the sleeves rolled up and displaying his muscular arms, with their black curly hair, up to his elbows. Apparently it was only the first three floors that had chamber maids. The coffee was better than one might have expected, but what use was that if there were no maids in white caps? That was a disappointment, and I wondered if there might not be some possibility of transferring to the third floor.

IV

Phoebus Böhlaug sits before a gleaming copper samovar eating scrambled egg and ham and drinking tea with milk. 'My doctor has prescribed eggs,' he says as he wipes his moustache on his serviette and, from his chair, stretches forth his face for me to kiss. The face smells of shaving soap and eau de Cologne. A smooth face, soft and warm. He wears an ample bath robe; he must have just come out of his tub. There is a newspaper lying on a chair, and a heart-shaped segment of his hirsute chest is on view, as he hasn't yet put on his shirt.

'You're looking fine!' he declares, with firm finality. 'How long have you been here?'

'Since yesterday!'

'So why come today?'

'I was here yesterday, but I could hear you were entertaining, and with this suit on I didn't want to...'

'What nonsense – it's a perfectly good suit! These days no one needs to be ashamed of anything. These days you won't find a millionaire in a better suit than that. I only have three suits myself. A suit costs a fortune!'

'I didn't know that's how things were. I've been a prisoner of war. I've just got out.'

'Did you have a good time there? By all accounts things are all right for prisoners.'

'There were some bad times too, Uncle Phoebus!'

'Aha. Well then, now you're going to be moving on from here?'

'Yes, and I need money.'

'I need money too,' Phoebus Böhlaug laughed. 'All of us need money.'

'You probably have some already.'

'I do? How do you know I do? Having to run for my life and then come back again and somehow getting my affairs back together again? I gave your father money back in Vienna – his illness cost me a tidy sum, and I paid for a gravestone for your dear mother, and a nice one it was too – that cost a good two thousand or so even then.'

'My father died in a hospice for incurables.'

'But your dear departed mother was in a sanatorium.'

'Why are you shouting like that? Don't get so excited, Phoebus!' says Regina, who now appears from the bedroom with a corset in her hand and her garters dangling down.

'This is Gabriel,' Phoebus introduces me.

Regina received a kiss on the hand. She expressed sympathy for me, for my suffering during captivity, about the war, the times we live in, about young people, and about her husband.

'Our little Alexander is with us, otherwise we'd have asked you to stay with us,' she says. Their young Alexander enters in blue pyjamas, gives a bow, clicks his slippered heels together. In the war he had made a timely move from the cavalry to the army service corps. Now he was studying in Paris – 'exports', as Phoebus put it – and was at home for the vacation.

'You're residing at the Savoy, I believe?' he asks, with all the assurance of a man of the world. 'There's a beautiful girl staying there,' – and he gives a wink for his father's benefit. 'She's called Stasia, and she's a dancer at the Varieté – you can't get anywhere near her, let me add – I wanted to take her with me to Paris' – he draws a little closer – 'but she's going there alone, when it suits her, so she says. A fine young girl!'

I stayed for lunch. Phoebus' daughter came with her husband. The son-in-law, apparently 'helping with the business', seemed a solid, good-natured type, sandy-haired, bull-necked; he spooned down his soup heartily, taking care to leave his plate spotless, and remained silent and quite unperturbed by the waves of conversation welling around him.

'I am just thinking,' said Regina, 'that blue suit of yours would fit Gabriel.'

'You mean I still have blue suits?' asked Phoebus.

'Yes,' said Regina. 'I'll go and get it.'

I tried in vain to resist. Alexander patted me on the shoulder. 'Quite right!' said the son-in-law, and Regina came back with the blue suit. I try it on in Alexander's room, in front of the large mirror. It does fit.

I gratefully acknowledge the need for a blue suit, 'as new', as well as the need for brown-spotted ties, and a brown waistcoat, and take my leave in the afternoon with a cardboard box under my arm. I promise to come back. Inside me there still whispers the faint hope of travel money.

'See? I've got him fitted out now,' says Phoebus to Regina.

V

The girl's name is Stasia. The Varieté theatre programme doesn't mention her name. She performs on cheap boards before 'young Alexanders' of the home-grown and the Parisian mould. She does a few turns in an oriental dance, then sits with her legs crossed in front of an incense-holder and waits for the end of the act. One can see her body, blue shadows under the arms, the swelling contour of a brown breast, the curve of the hip, the upper thigh emerging from the abrupt edge of her short tricot.

There was a ludicrous group of brass players, and no violins – almost painful. There were old comic songs, some rotten old jokes from a clown, a trained donkey, with the ends of its ears dyed red, that long-sufferingly minced up and down, white-clad waiters smelling like beer-cellars carrying overflowing frothing mugs between the darkened rows, the glare of a yellow spotlight shining obliquely out of an arbitrarily placed opening in the ceiling, a gloomy stage backcloth like a gaping, screaming mouth, the compère's rasping voice announcing grim tidings.

I wait by the stage door. It's just like the old days when I was a boy and used to wait in the little side street, huddled back in the shadow of a gateway and blending into it, until I heard quick young footsteps ringing out, issuing from the pavement, wondrously blossoming out of the barren cobblestones.

When Stasia came out she was with men and women, a jumble of mingling voices.

For a long time I was lonely, surrounded by thousands. Now there are a thousand things I can share: the sight of a crooked gable roof, a swallow's nest in the cupboard at the Hotel Savoy, the irritating yellow eyes of the ageing lift-boy, the abjectness of the seventh floor, the weirdness of a Greek name and a grammatical concept suddenly brought to life, unhappy memories of a spiteful old aorist and the cramped smallness of my parental home, the inflated, ridiculous figure of Phoebus Böhlaug, and the life-saving move of their dear little Alex to the service corps. Living things became more alive, things commonly condemned became more hateful, Heaven closer, the world now subject to me.

The door of the lift was open; Stasia was sitting there. I did not hide my joy; we wished each other good evening like old acquaintances. I greeted the unavoidable lift-boy grudgingly. He affected not to know that I had to get out at the sixth floor, and took us both up to the seventh. Stasia got out here and vanished into her room, while the lift-boy lingered, as if he had to collect some passengers up here. What's he waiting for, with those spiteful yellow eyes of his?

So I go slowly downstairs, listening for the lift to start again. Finally – I am half way down – I hear the gurgling sound of the lift, and turn round. Up on the top floor the fellow is starting on his way down the stairs; he has sent the lift down empty, and he's making his own laboured, ill-tempered way down on foot.

Stasia has probably been waiting for my knock on the door.

I want to apologise.

'No, no,' says Stasia. 'I would have invited you before, but I was afraid of Ignatz. He is the most dangerous person in the Hotel Savoy. And I also know your name, Gabriel Dan, and I know you've just been released – yesterday I thought you were a – a colleague – an artiste–' she hesitates – perhaps she is afraid of offending me?

I was not offended. 'No,' I said, 'I don't really know what I am. There was a time I wanted to become a writer, but then I went to the war, and now I don't think there's any point in writing. – I am a solitary soul, and I'm not able to write for other people.

'You're living just above my room,' I said, not being able to think of anything cleverer. 'Why do you walk around all night?'

'I'm learning French. I'm hoping to go to Paris, and do something real, not just dance. There was a silly oaf who wanted to take me to Paris with him; that's how I got the idea of going there.'

'Alexander Böhlaug?'

'You know him? And you only got here yesterday?'

'Well, you've already got to know me.'

'Have you also talked to Ignatz?'

'No, but Böhlaug is my cousin.'

'Oh! I'm sorry.'

'No, no, please, he really is a silly oaf.'

Stasia has some bars of chocolate. She produces a spirit stove out of the bottom of a hatbox.

'Nobody must know about this. Even Ignatz doesn't know about it. I hide this stove somewhere different every day. Today it's the hatbox, yesterday I wrapped it up in my muff, and once I hid it behind the cupboard. The police don't allow spirit stoves in hotels. But we – I mean people like us – can't live anywhere else, and the Savoy is the best I know. Are you going to be staying here long?'

'No, just a few days.'

'Oh, then you won't get to know the Savoy. Santschin and his family are living just next door. He's our clown – would you like to meet him?'

I'm not that keen. But Stasia needs tea.

The Santschins don't in fact live 'just next door', but at the other end of the corridor near the laundry. Here the ceiling is sloping, and hangs down so low that you're afraid you'll bump your head on it. In reality, however, there's quite a distance between you and it – it just looks so threatening. Generally, in this corner all the dimensions seem restricted; it's because of the grey steam that comes out of the laundry room and blinds the eye, reduces distances and makes the walls swell out. It's hard to get used to this constantly seething air obscuring the outlines of things, smelling dank and warm, transforming people into a of blur unreal forms.

There's steam even inside Santschin's room. His wife closes the door hurriedly after we enter, as if there's a wild animal lying in wait out there. They've been in this room for six months, and have had plenty of practice at closing the door quickly. Their lamp burns in a circle of grey light, reminding me of photographs of constellations with surrounding nebulae. Santschin stands up, slips an arm into a dark-coloured jacket, and acknowledges his guests with a nod. His head seems to emerge from clouds, like the head of some spiritual apparition in a religious painting,

He is smoking a long pipe and says little. The pipe prevents him from conversing properly. Having managed to compose half a sentence, he has to pause, reach for his wife's knitting needle and start poking around in the bowl of the pipe. Or else he has to strike another match, and that means searching for the matchbox, but Frau Santschin is heating milk for the child and needs the matches herself, just as often as her husband needs them. The box commutes incessantly from Santschin's side to the washstand, where the spirit stove is standing, and sometimes gets left somewhere on the way and vanishes without trace in the misty blur. Santschin bends down and knocks over a chair, the milk boils and is removed from the stove while the flame continues to burn until something that needs heating is put on – the danger being that the matchbox has now disappeared for good.

I proffered my own box of matches to husband and wife in turns – but neither would take it, both of them apparently preferring to continue the search, and to leave the stove purposelessly burning away. In the end it was Stasia who found the matches in a fold of the bedspread.

A second later Frau Santschin is searching for the keys so she can get the tea out of the trunk – 'after all', it could always be stolen from the caddy. 'I can hear rattling somewhere,' says Santschin in Russian, and we all stand still to see if we can catch the rattling of the keys. But not a sound. 'Well, they can't just rattle on their own,' Santschin exclaims. 'You've all got to move, then we'll soon hear them!'

But the first we heard of them was when Frau Santschin discovered a milk stain on her blouse and hastily snatched up her apron in order to avoid staining it a second time. As it turns out, the keys have been in the apron pocket all the time. But in the trunk there isn't even a grain of tea dust left. 'You're looking for the tea?' asks Santschin suddenly. 'I finished it this morning!'

'Why are you sitting there like a great lump and not saying anything?' his wife bellows at him.

'For a start, I've not been silent,' replies Santschin, ever the logician. 'And secondly, nobody's asking me anyway. You see, Herr Dan, you should understand that I count last in this household.'

Frau Santschin had an idea: tea could be bought from Herr Fisch – that is, if he was awake at the time. There was no certain prospect of his lending any tea, but if there were some 'advantage' to him he would be only too glad to sell some. 'Let's go and see Fisch,' says Stasia.

Fisch has to be woken first. He lives in the last room in the hotel, no. 864, *gratis*, since he is paid for by the town's tradespeople and industrialists and the distinguished residents on the lower floors of the Savoy. The story goes that he was once married and well respected, a manufacturer, and wealthy. In the course of time he lost all of this through carelessness, but who knows? He lives on the discreet charity of others, but without admitting it; he calls himself a 'lottery dreamer'. He has the gift of dreaming lottery numbers which cannot fail to come up. He sleeps through the day, to allow the numbers to appear, then places his bets. But before they are drawn he's already had another dream; whereupon he sells his ticket, buys another one on the proceeds, then the old one wins and the new one doesn't. Many have become rich thanks to Fisch's dreams, and now live on the first floor. In gratitude they pay for Fisch's room.

Fisch – his first name is Hirsch – lives in constant fear; he once read somewhere that the government are going to do away with the lottery and bring in a lucky-draw system.

Hirsch Fisch must have been dreaming some 'nice numbers' on this occasion, since it is a good while before he stirs. He doesn't allow anyone into his room, receives me in the corridor, duly listens to Stasia's request, slams the door again, then after a considerable time opens it, with a little packet of tea in his hand.

'We'll put it on the account, Herr Fisch,' says Stasia.

'Good evening,' says Fisch, and retires to bed.

'If you have any money,' Stasia advises me, 'buy yourself a lottery ticket from Fisch' – and she tells me about the Jew's miraculous dreams.'

I laugh – I am ashamed to confess I have any belief in miracles, to which I am easy prey. I am, though, determined to buy a ticket the moment Fisch offers me one.

The fortunes of Santschin and Fisch preoccupied me. Everyone in this place seemed to be cloaked in secrets. Was I just dreaming? What about the steam from the laundry? What was living there behind this door, or that one? Who had built this hotel? Who was this Kalegyropoulos, the proprietor?

'Do you know Kalegyropoulos?'

Stasia did not know him. No one knew him. No one had ever seen him. But if you had the time and the inclination you could lie in wait just as he was coming round to inspect, and take a look at him.

'Glanz tried it once,' Stasia said, 'but he didn't get to see him. By the way, Ignatz says there's an inspection tomorrow.'

Before I get downstairs Hirsch Fisch catches up with me, wearing a shirt and white long johns. Before him he holds, stiffly and at some distance, a chamber pot. Tall and gaunt, in this murky twilight he looks as if he's just risen from the tomb. The grey stubble on his face bristles and menaces, like tiny sharp spears, his deep sunken eyes overshadowed by prominent cheekbones.

'Good morning, Herr Dan! Do you think the young lady will pay me for the tea?'

'Well, it's most likely isn't it?'

'Listen, I've dreamt some numbers! An absolute certainty! I'll be betting on them today. Have you heard that the government's intending to stop the lottery?'

'No!'

'It would be a terrible misfortune, I'm telling you. What are ordinary folk supposed to live on? How can they ever hope to become rich? Are we supposed to wait for some old aunt to die? Or a grandfather? Just to find in the will that everything's going to the orphanage.'

Fisch talks on, holding the chamber pot out in front of him, apparently having forgotten that it's there. I eye it, which he notices.

'You know, I save on tips. What do I need room service for? I keep my own things in order. People here are a bunch of thieving magpies. Everyone's lost something by now, except me that is! No, I've got everything in order. Today, according to Ignatz, it's inspection. I always make sure I'm out – if you're not there, you're not there. If Kalegyropoulos finds something wrong, he's not going to pin it on me. Am I his trainee?'

'Do you know the proprietor?'

'Why should I know him? I've no interest in getting to anyone else. Have you heard the latest? Bloomfield's coming!'

'Who's Bloomfield?'

'You don't know Bloomfield? He is a son of this town, a millionaire in America. The whole town is buzzing with it:

'Bloomfield's coming!' I'm telling you, I've actually spoken with his father, I really have – just as close as we are now!'

'Forgive me, Herr Fisch, I need to get a little more sleep.'

'Oh, please, please. Sleep! I have to clear up anyway.' Fisch heads off towards the toilet. But he turned back half way and ran after me when I was already on my way down:

'Do you think she's going to pay?'

'Absolutely certain.'

I opened the door of my room, and once again, just like the day before, I felt I saw a scurrying shadow. I was too tired to go and look. I slept until the sun was far up in the sky.

VI

It resounded through the whole building like a clarion call: Kalegyropoulos is on the way! He always came in the early evening before sunset – a veritable creature of the twilight, Lord of the Bats. Women stood strategically in place on the three upper floors scrubbing the stones. One could clearly hear the splashing of floor-mops in filled buckets, the scrubbing of hard brooms and the soothing swish of dry cloths sweeping the corridor. There's a bedroom waiter, yellow bottle of cleaning fluid in his hand, polishing all the door handles.

Lights twinkle, push-buttons and door-fittings glisten, steam gushes even more copiously from the laundry, and creeps down onto the sixth floor. Men in dark blue stand up by the ceiling on swaying ladders, testing the electric wiring through gloved hands. Maids with billowing skirts hang like human flags out of the windows, polishing the glass panes. Up on the seventh floor all the inhabitants have disappeared, the doors stand open, exposing to view all their wretched domesticity – hastily assembled bundles and heaps of newspapers concealing forbidden objects.

On the respectable floors the chamber maids wear splendidly stiffened coifs, smelling of starch and the excitement of festivities, just like a Sunday morning; it surprises me that there are no church bells ringing. Down there someone is wiping the palms of his hands with a handkerchief; it's the manager himself, his eye fixed on a leather armchair with a tear in the seat revealing its innards of wood-shavings. The porter quickly covers it over with a mat.

Two bookkeepers stand behind high cash desks recording accounts, one of them going through the pages of the register. The porter sports a new gold braid round the edge of his cap. A servant steps out of a little cubicle in a new green apron, verdant as a meadow in spring. Corpulent men sit in the lobby smoking and drinking schnapps, busy waiters hovering around them.

I order a schnapps and sit down at a table out at the edge of the lobby, right next to the carpet runner over which Kalegyropoulos presumably has to make his entrance. Ignatz walks coolly by, gives an unusually friendly nod, his demeanour quite out of place for a lift-boy. He seems to be the only one in the hotel to maintain this calm, his clothes apparently unchanged, his clean-shaven face, a bluish sheen at the chin, today every bit as pastor-like as ever.

I waited half an hour. Suddenly I saw movement at the front in the porter's office, the manager reached for the cash ledger, brandished it on high like a signal for something, and ran up the steps. A fat hotel guest put down the schnapps glass which he had just half raised, and asked the man next to him, 'What's going on?' The latter, a Russian, replied uninterestedly, 'Kalegyropoulos is on the first floor.'

How had he got there?

On the bedside table in my room I found a bill with an extra note stamped on it:

'Our honoured guests are politely requested to pay in cash.

Cheques are on principle not accepted. Respectfully, Kalegyro-poulos, Proprietor.'

The manager came a quarter of an hour later and apologised, saying this was an error and the bill had been meant for another guest who had requested it. The manager took his leave. He was most upset; his apologies were endless, as if he'd condemned an innocent man to death and was overwhelmed with remorse. He made one more bow, a deep one, as his hand was on the door handle, concealing the bill sheepishly in the tails of his coat.

Later the house came alive, a beehive of residents all swarming in with their honeyed riches. Hirsch Fisch was with them, and the Santschin family, and many others I didn't know; and Stasia too. She was afraid to enter her room.

'Why are you afraid?'

'There's a bill there,' she said, 'and I can't pay it. Ignatz will have to come back with the patent.'

I asked what kind of 'patent' she meant.

'Later,' she said. She was very flustered. She was wearing a thin blouse, and I could see her tiny breasts.

On her bedside table there was a bill. It was a considerable amount. If I had wanted to pay it, it would have swallowed easily half my cash.

Stasia soon recovered. In front of the mirror she found a bouquet, carnations and summer flowers.

'The flowers are from Alexander Böhlaug,' she said, 'but I never send flowers back. What can the flowers do about it?'

Then she sent for Ignatz.

Ignatz arrived, with a searching look on his face, and bowed deeply in front of me.

'Your patent, Ignatz,' says Stasia.

Ignatz produces a chain from his trouser pocket and reaches for a toiletry case in front of the mirror.

'The third one,' says Ignatz and winds the chain round the case four times. He does so with a prurient look, as if it is Stasia he is tying up rather than her case. He fastens a little lock on the ends of the chain, then folds the bill and slips it inside his tattered wallet. Ignatz lends money to anyone who has cases. He pays the bills of those who agree to pawn their luggage with him. The suitcases remain in their owners' rooms, locked up by Ignatz and unable to be opened. The 'patent' lock is his own invention. He comes every morning to see that 'his' cases remain untouched.

Stasia makes do with just two dresses. She's already pawned three trunks. I resolve to buy one trunk, and think to myself it would be best to leave Hotel Savoy quickly.

I no longer liked the hotel: not the suffocating laundry, not the sinister benevolence of the lift-boy, not the three floors of prisoners. It was like the world itself, this Hotel Savoy, shining out brilliantly and pouring its lustre from all seven floors, while poverty dwelt inside in its lofty heights, and that life up there on high was the life of the downcast, buried in ethereal graves, graves stacked up in layers above the luxurious quarters of the well-fed who sat down there in cosy serenity, unburdened by the insubstantial coffins up above them.

I belong among those people there in their lofty graves. Am I not living just on the sixth floor? Not yet the eighth, the tenth, the twentieth? How high can one still fall? Into Heaven, into eternal bliss?

'You are so far away from us,' says Stasia.

'Forgive me,' I plead; her voice has moved me.

VII

Phoebus Böhlaug never failed to refer to the blue suit, calling it 'a perfect gem of a suit', and 'as if made to measure', and smiling. Once at my uncle's I met Glanz, Abel Glanz, a small, shabbily dressed, unshaved individual who contracted fearfully into himself whenever you spoke to him; he had a talent for becoming automatically smaller, by virtue of some mysterious innate mechanism. His thin neck and restlessly rolling Adam's apple could concertina together and disappear beneath his wide standing collar. Only his forehead was of any appreciable size; his hair was thin on top and his red ears jutted far out, giving the impression they had adopted this position precisely so as to allow everyone the privilege of studying them. Abel Glanz's little eyes looked at me venomously. Perhaps he viewed me as a rival.

Abel Glanz has been visiting Phoebus Böhlaug's house for years, one of those constant teatime guests that the well-to-do households of the town are terrified will be their undoing and yet can never summon up the courage to show the door.

'Do have a cup of tea,' said Phoebus Böhlaug.

'No thank you,' replies Abel Glanz. 'I'm as full up with tea as a samovar. That's already the fourth cup I've had to turn down, Mr Böhlaug. I've been drinking tea the whole time ever since I finished my lunch. Please don't force me, Mr Böhlaug!'

Böhlaug is not to be dissuaded.

'You won't have had a better cup of tea in your life, Glanz.'

'But what can you be thinking, Mr Böhlaug! I once had an invitation from Princess Basikoff, Mr Böhlaug, don't forget that!' says Abel Glanz, as imposingly as is possible for him.

'And I'm telling you, even the Princess Basikoff herself never drank such tea as this! Ask my son if there's such a tea to be found in the whole of Paris.'

'You think so?' says Abel Glanz, and pretends to be pondering the question.

'Well, then one may as well have a taste, tasting can't do any harm.' And he shifts his chair closer to the samovar.

Abel Glanz was previously a prompter at a small-time Romanian theatre, but he felt his calling was more that of a director and he couldn't endure having to sit there in his prompter's box watching people making 'mistakes'. Glanz privileged all and sundry with his life story. Once he'd managed to be given a trial run directing a play. A week later he was called up, and they put him in the ambulance corps because some sergeant had thought that the profession of 'prompting' had something to do with medicine.

'That's the kind of game Fate plays with people,' Abel Glanz concluded.

'Glanz is also living at the Savoy,' Böhlaug said once, and I had the feeling my uncle intended some comparison between me and the prompter. As far as Böhlaug was concerned we belonged in the same category, both of us vaguely 'artists', and more or less spongers, though to be fair one should admit that at least the prompter was making some genuine effort to take up a respectable profession. He wanted to be a merchant, and that was best done by 'doing business'.

'You know, Glanz does some quite good business deals,' says Uncle Phoebus.

'What kind of business?'

'Currency,' says Phoebus Böhlaug, 'it's certainly dangerous, but it's a sure deal. It's just a matter of luck. If you don't have luck on your side you may as well forget it, but if you have got it you can be a millionaire in no time.'

'Uncle, why don't you deal in currency?'

'God forbid!' cries Phoebus. 'I don't want anything to do with the police! It's only when you've got nothing, that's when you deal in currency.'

'You think Phoebus Böhlaug should deal in currency?' asks Abel Glanz, and the question suggests deep indignation.

'It is not at all easy dealing in currency,' says Abel Glanz. 'You're risking your neck – it's a Jewish fate. You spend the whole day running around. If you need Romanian lei, you find there's nothing but Swiss francs on offer, and if its francs you're after, then there's only lei. It's quite uncanny! Your uncle's telling you I do good business? The rich man always thinks everyone's doing good business.'

'So who's told you I'm a rich man?' says Phoebus.

'Who needs to tell me? I don't need to be told by anyone. The whole world knows – If Böhlaug's signed, that counts as money.

'Well the world's a liar!' bellows Böhlaug, and his voice suddenly rises in pitch, shouting as if 'the world' had accused him of some awful crime.

Young Alexander entered at this point, wearing a fashionable suit, and a yellow net on his sleekly coiffed hair, reeking of all manner of things, of mouthwash and brilliantine, and smoking a sweet-scented cigarette.

'There's no disgrace in having money, father,' he says.

'You're right,' cried Glanz gleefully. 'Your father *is* ashamed!'

Phoebus Böhlaug poured some more tea. 'There are your own children for you!' he groaned.

Phoebus Böhlaug has at this moment become an old man, ashen-faced, wrinkles over his eyelids, shoulders hunched forward, as if suddenly metamorphosed.

'Life isn't that good for any of us,' he says. 'You work and toil away your whole life, just to be buried in the end.'

It has suddenly turned very still. And evening is already drawing in.

'We need light!' says Böhlaug.

This was meant for Glanz.

'I'll be going now. Many thanks for the excellent tea!'

Phoebus Böhlaug offers him his hand and turns to me: 'And you too should come a little more often.'

Glanz led me through unfamiliar alleys, past courtyards and neglected enclosures and empty lots covered in muck and dirt, pigs grunting and rooting about for fodder with their filthy snouts. Swarms of green flies buzzed around heaps of dark brown human excrement. The town had no drains, and there was a stench coming from every house, and Glanz prophesied sudden rain on the basis of this miscellany of all kinds of odours.

'That's how things go for us,' says Glanz. 'Böhlaug's a rich man with a small heart. You see, Herr Dan, it's not that people have a *bad* heart, it's just far too small. It can't manage that much, just about enough for wife and children.'

We arrive at a small lane. There are Jews standing around here and walking about in the middle of the street with ridiculously rolled umbrellas with crooked handles. They are either standing still with pensive expressions or endlessly walking up and down. Here one of them disappears, there another one comes out of a doorway, looks searchingly to left and right, and begins to stroll around.

The people pass each other like silent shadows. This is a collection of phantoms; this is where people long dead walk about; for thousands of years this tribe have frequented these narrow lanes.

When we come closer we see two of them stop, murmur something, pass by again without greeting each other, only to meet again a few minutes later and exchange another murmured half-sentence.

A policeman appears in squeaking yellow boots. With his sabre swinging he marches right up the middle of the street, past some Jews who stand aside for him, greet him, call out something to him, and smile. No greeting, no call will halt him, and he strides on with measured steps, up the street like a wound-up machine. His movement hasn't caused the slightest alarm.

'Streimer is coming,' someone whispers at Abel Glanz's side. And there he is, Jakob Streimer himself.

At that moment a man in blue overalls lights a gas lamp, and it seems as if this is in honour of the guests.

Abel Glanz grows uneasy – as do all the Jews.

Jakob Streimer is waiting at the end of the street. He is waiting for the approaching crowd, standing even more imposingly than the policeman; he stands like an oriental prince giving audience to a delegation of petitioning subjects. He has a gold-rimmed pince-nez and well-tended whiskers, and a top hat.

Word was soon circulating that Jakob Streimer needed German reichsmarks.

Abel Glanz went into a shop, in which a woman was apparently waiting for customers. The woman withdrew from her post, a door opened, a bell rang, a man stepped out of the shop.

Glanz was soon back, and was radiant: 'I got marks for eleven and three eighths. Ah, you like that, don't you! Streimer's paying twelve and three quarters!'

I am about to question him, but Glanz just slips his hand into my inside pocket, and with disconcerting dexterity he draws out my wallet, takes out all the notes, thrusts a bundle of crumpled bank notes into my hand and says, 'Come with me.'

'Ten thousand,' he says and stops in front of Jakob Streimer.

'This gentleman?' asks Streimer.

'Yes, Herr Dan.' Streimer nods.

'Savoy,' he says.

'I congratulate you, Mr Dan,' says Glanz, 'Streimer has invited you.'

'How so?'

'Didn't you hear? He said "Savoy". Let's be going. If your uncle Phoebus Böhlaug had a warm heart you'd be able to go and borrow money from him, and then buy yourself some German marks – within two hours you'd be a hundred thousand better off. But *he* won't be giving you a penny. So you've earned yourself a princely five thousand.'

'That's quite a bit too!'

'Nothing's quite a bit. Quite a bit – a billion would be quite a bit,' says Glanz. 'These days there's no such thing as "quite a bit". Can anyone tell what tomorrow will bring? Tomorrow it's a revolution. And the day after – the Bolsheviks will be here. The old fairy tales have come true. Today you have a hundred thousand in your safe, and by the time you get there tomorrow it's fifty thousand. We're actually seeing that kind of miracle these days – not even money's still money! What more do you want than that!'

We came to the Savoy. Glanz opened a small door at the end of the corridor, and there was Ignatz.

It was a bar, in a room painted dark red. A red-haired woman was standing at the bar, and a there were a few dolled up girls sitting around the room at small tables, drinking lemonade through thin straws.

Glanz said hello, 'Good day to you, Frau Kupfer,' and introduced me: 'Herr Dan – Frau Jetti Kupfer, our Alma Mater.'

'That's Latin,' he explains to Frau Kupfer.

'Yes, I know, you're an educated man,' says Frau Kupfer, 'but you've got to earn more money, Herr Glanz.'

'Now she's getting even with me, for my Latin.' Glanz feels ashamed.

The room was half dark. In one corner there was a reddish glow from a lamp and a black grand piano stood in front of a small stage.

I drank two schnapps and sank into a leather armchair. In front of the bar there were some men sitting and eating bread and caviar. A piano player sat down at the instrument.

VIII

We are sitting at small tables. They all seem to know each other here; it's one big family. Frau Jetti Kupfer rings a little silver bell, whereupon some naked women step out onto the stage. All goes quiet and dark, chairs are moved round, eyes set on the stage. The girls are young, powdered white. They dance poorly, each writhes to the music in whatever way pleases her. Out of all of them – there are ten – I notice one, a little, frail girl with freckles scrupulously powdered over and frightened blue eyes. Her small bones look fragile, her movements awkward and nervous; her hands try vainly to hide her breasts, which are small and pointed and constantly tremble like shivering animals.

Then a second ring from Frau Jetti on the silver bell, and the dancing stops, the pianist thunders forth with a fanfare, the light glares out, and all the female bodies recede together half a step, as if it was only the raised light that had stripped them. They all turn and trip off in single file, and Frau Jetti Kupfer shouts, 'Toni!'

Toni was the little one with freckles, and on she came. Frau Jetti Kupfer left the bar counter as if coming down from the clouds, spreading around her a strong smell of perfume and liquor. She makes the introduction: Fräulein Toni, our latest addition!'

'Bravo!' shouted a gentleman – it was Herr Kanner, an aniline manufacturer, as Glanz explained to me. 'Tonka,' he said, making a sign of approbation with his thumb and index finger, and his left hand reached out to try to touch Tonka's hips.

'Where have the girls got to?' shouted Jakob Streimer. 'What kind of service do call this? You've got Herr Neuner and Herr Anselm Schwadron sitting here, and they're being treated like – well, who knows who…!' Ignatz glided across the room bringing over five of the naked girls, and distributed them round different tables. Frau Kupfer said, 'We weren't reckoning on so many guests.'

Anselm Schwadron and Philipp Neuner, the manufacturers, both stood up at once, beckoned two of the girls over to them, and ordered prunelle cocktails.

A guest walked in, greeted with much acclamation from all sides, and the girls appeared quite forgotten, sitting on their diminutive little chairs like unwanted surplus goods.

The new arrival calls out, 'Bloomfield's in Berlin today!'

'Berlin today!' they all echo.

'When's he coming?' asks Kanner, the aniline man.

'He could be here any day!' the newcomer replies.

'And it would be now that my workers have to go on strike!' says Philipp Neuner, a German, large, reddish blond hair, bull-necked, with strong, round childlike features.

'Come to terms with them, Neuner!' shouts Kanner.

'Twenty percent pay rise for married workers?' asks Neuner. 'Can *you* pay that?'

'I always give a pay rise for every new child born,' Kanner rejoins, 'and since I started, we've had a right old outbreak of new babies. I only wish all my enemies had such a productive workforce! These fellows are fooling themselves, I keep telling them, but a worker can lose his senses over two percent extra pay and saddle me with a truckload of children.'

'Here we go again,' says Streimer wearily.

'A manufacturer isn't an estate agent! Just remember that!' snarls Philipp Neuner. Neuner once served for a year with the Guards.

'A dueller,' says Glanz.

'More that than a manufacturer,' says Streimer, 'but we're not in Prussia.'

Ignatz comes rushing in with a telegram. For a few seconds he enjoys the silence and suspense he has created, then says, so softly that they can hardly make out his words,

'A telegram from Herr Bloomfield. He arrives on Thursday; he's booking room 13!'

'Thirteen? – Bloomfield's superstitious,' Kanner explains.

'We only have 12A and 14,' says Ignatz.

'Paint on a number thirteen then,' says Jakob Streimer.

'I love it! Bravo, Streimer!' shouts Neuner, pacified and holding out his hand to Streimer.

'It's the estate agent in me,' says Streimer, quickly putting his hand in his trouser pocket.

'Now no disputes here, please,' Kanner intervenes, 'not when Bloomfield's on the way!'

I go up to the seventh floor; I have a sudden feeling that Stasia has to be there to meet me. But Hirsch Fisch steps out of his room, chamber pot in hand.

'Bloomfield's coming! Would you believe it?'

I am no longer listening.

IX

Santschin has suddenly been taken ill.

'Suddenly,' everyone is saying, without realising that Santschin has been constantly on the point of death for the last ten years. Day in, day out. In the Simbirsk prison camp a year ago a man suddenly dropped dead like that. A little Jewish fellow. It happened one afternoon while he was cleaning his mess kit – just fell down dead. He lay face down with arms and legs stretched out – dead. Somebody said at the time, 'Ephraim Krojanker has suddenly died.'

'Number 748 has suddenly fallen ill,' say the room servants. There were no names at all on the upper three floors of the hotel. The people were all known by room numbers.

Number 748 is Santschin, Vladimir Santschin. He is lying on the bed half dressed, smoking, and doesn't want a doctor.

'It's a family illness,' he says. 'It's the lungs. There was a chance mine might have remained healthy; when I was born I was a sturdy little chap and yelled so loud the midwife had to plug her ears. But out of malice, and perhaps because there was no other place in that tiny room, she put me on the windowsill. I've been coughing ever since.'

Santschin lies there barefoot on the bed, with nothing but his trousers on. I notice his feet are dirty and his toes are ravaged by corns and all kinds of unnatural disfigurements. His feet remind me of strange forest tree roots. His big toes are gnarled and knobbly.

He doesn't want a doctor, because his grandfather and his father also died without a doctor.

Hirsch Fisch arrives and offers him a medicinal tea, hoping to sell it at a 'reasonable' price.

When he sees that no one wants the tea he asks me to come out of the room: 'Perhaps you'd like to buy a lottery ticket?'

'Let's see it,' I say.

'The draw's next Friday. You can be absolutely sure of these numbers.' The numbers were 5, 8 and 3.

Stasia runs past us, out of breath, unable even to wait for Ignatz and the lift. Her face is flushed, and strands of hair flutter all around it.

'You have to give me some money, Herr Fisch,' she says. 'Herr Santschin must have a doctor.'

'Then buy the tea too,' says Fisch, stealing a glance in my direction.

'I'll pay the doctor,' I say, and buy the tea.

'Keep calm, Herr Santschin,' I say in Russian. 'Stasia has gone for the doctor.'

'Why don't they tell me?' Santschin flares up. I ease him, with some effort, back onto the bed. 'We've got to open the windows, woman, do you hear me? And empty out the bucket, and get rid of the ash! The doctor's going to go on at me about the smoking, of course. All doctors are the same about that. And another thing, I haven't shaved. Give me my razor – it's there on the chest of drawers.'

But the razor is not there on the chest of drawers. Frau Santschin finds it in amongst her sewing things; she's been using it instead of scissors to remove trouser buttons.

I have to give Santschin a glass of water; he wets his face, takes a little mirror out of his trouser pocket and holds it in front of him in his left hand, contorts his mouth, sticks his tongue into his right cheek to make the skin taut, and shaves without soap. He cuts himself only once – 'because you're watching me,' he says, and I feel ashamed and look away into one of the corners of the room.

'Now the doctor can come.'

I knew this doctor. He used to sit in the tea room of the hotel every day. He is a former army doctor. His long service shows clearly; he has that firm, resounding tread of the former officer, and the pronounced upper torso.

Even now he still wears little spurs on his heels, despite the otherwise civilian dress and ordinary trousers. His upright posture, metallic eyes and overpowering voice radiate an air of Imperial manoeuvres.

'Only the South can save you,' says the doctor. 'But if you don't get to the South, the South must come to you. Just one moment...'

The doctor strides noisily over the door and rings the bell. He keeps his finger on the bell and continues to ring while speaking. It takes a few minutes for the waiter to arrive and knock at the door.

The room servant stands stiffly to attention before the doctor, who shouts his order in his most practised officer's tone: 'Bring me the wine list!'

For a while the room goes very quiet; Santschin's eyes wander inquisitively, probingly, from the doctor to Stasia, to me. Then the waiter arrives with the wine list. 'One bottle of Malaga and five glasses, on my bill,' the doctor orders.

'No other medicine,' he says peremptorily to Santschin. 'Three small glasses each day, do you understand me?'

The doctor pours the wine into all five glasses, half filling them, and hands them out one by one. As he does so, I notice his age. His bony hands are covered in little blue veins, and they tremble.

'Your very good health!' says the doctor to Santschin, and we all touch glasses. It feels like some kind of cheerful funeral wake.

I hand the old doctor his hat and stick, and Stasia and I go along the corridor with him.

'He won't survive more than two bottles,' said the doctor. 'Still, there's no need to tell him that! He doesn't need to make a will.'

The doctor struck his heavy stick against the flagstones, and strode off with spurs ringing out. He wouldn't take any money.

That evening I went with Stasia to the Varieté.

It was still the same programme, only there was something missing, or did it just seem so to me because I was feeling Santschin's absence? His donkey trotted on stage with the red painted hairs on its long ears which it kept moving up and down like handles on springs. The donkey was looking for something on the stage – he was missing Santschin, Santschin the cheerful joker, Santschin who curled his body up in a ball on the boards, Santschin with his husky, croaking voice and funny clucks and whoops and circus weeping and bawling. The donkey felt uneasy, throwing up his forelegs and dancing on his back legs to a march from the brass players, then trotting off again.

I saw young Alex Böhlaug. He was sitting in the front row eating bread and caviar, which he held with his thumb and middle finger, splaying his child's hand. When the dance number started up and Stasia came on stage, his face suddenly tensed as if he was in some pain. But it was just because he was wedging in a monocle.

Then I went home with Stasia. We took the quiet backstreets, and could see through lighted windows into little rooms, all of them poor rooms with little Jewish children eating bread and radish and burying their faces in big gourds.

'Did you notice how sad August looked?'

'Who is August?'

'Santschin's donkey. He's been working with Santschin for six years.'

'Hotel Savoy is going to be one man the poorer now,' I said – merely because I was afraid to remain silent.

Stasia said nothing – she was waiting for me to say something else. Just as we are coming to the market square – we are in the last little lane – Stasia hesitates, and would happily have stayed there longer.

We spoke not another word until we were sitting in the lift with Ignatz; his watchful look embarrasses us, so we just chat superficially.

That night Stasia moved Frau Santschin's and the child's bedding into her own room, and asked me to stay with Santschin.

Santschin was happy. He thanked Stasia and took her hand and mine, and pressed them both.

It was a terrible night.

I remembered the nights I had spent out on those free, open snowfields, nights stationed on watch duty, white nights freezing in the snow on the Podolian plateau, and others lit up by the glare of rockets that furrowed glowing red wounds in the dark sky. But in my whole life there had never been any night so awful as this, not even the night when I myself was hovering uncertainly between life and death.

Santschin's temperature rises suddenly, rapidly. Stasia comes with towels soaked in vinegar, and we drape them round Santschin's head – it doesn't help.

Santschin is delirious. He gives a performance for free. He calls for August, his donkey. He calls him over gently, offers him his hand as if to offer the animal a sugar lump, as he does before every show. He leaps up and shouts. He claps his hands, as in the theatre, inviting approval, sticks his head forward, waggles his ears and then pricks them up like a dog and listens for the applause.

'Clap now,' says Stasia, and we all clap. Santschin takes a bow. Next morning Santschin lay in a cold sweat. The great drops were breaking out like glass boils on his forehead. There was a stench of vinegar and urine and foul air.

Frau Santschin wailed gently, pressing her head on the side of the door. We let her cry.

As I left with Stasia, Ignatz said good morning to us. He was standing in the corridor, looking as natural as if this, and nowhere else in the world, were his normal post.

'Santschin is going to die, then?' asked Ignatz.

At this moment I feel that death has taken on the shape of the old lift-boy, and is standing here right now, waiting for a soul.

X

Santschin was buried at three in the afternoon, in a remote part of the eastern cemetery.

If anyone wants to visit his grave in the winter he'll have to work hard and dig out a path with spade and shovel. All the graves of paupers buried at public expense are far off, and it will take three full generations to die before this distant part of the hallowed graveyard shows any sign of human presence.

But by then no one will be able to find Santschin's grave.

Not even Abel Glanz, the poor prompter, will be lying so far away.

Santschin's grave is cold and clayey – I looked in while he was being buried – and his remains are being surrendered, defenceless, to the creatures of the soil.

Santschin was kept at the theatre for three days, because the Savoy is not at all a hotel for the dead, but for the fully alive. He lay behind the stage in a clothes cupboard, and his wife sat beside him, with a poor sexton praying. The director of the theatre had contributed the candles.

The dancing girls had to pass the dead Santschin on their way onto the stage. The band did its worst as usual, and even August the donkey came that way, but Santschin did not stir.

None of the guests knew that there was a corpse lying behind the stage. The police had tried to forbid it at first, but one of their officers who was always given free seats – his relatives filled a quarter of the seats in the place – procured permission.

The cortège started out from the Varieté Theatre, and the director went with it as far as the edge of the town, where the slaughterhouses are – in this town the dead are taken on the same route as the animals. Santschin's colleagues, with Stasia and me and his wife, followed all the way to his grave.

When we reached the cemetery gate we found Xaver Zlotogor, the mesmerist, quarrelling with the cemetery manager. Zlotogor had brought Santschin's donkey to the open grave without being noticed, and left him standing there.

'He can't be buried like that!' shouted the manager.

'He is going to be buried like that!' said Zlotogor

There was a short hiatus; the priest was to settle the matter, which he did when Xaver Zlotogor whispered something in his ear – the animal could stay.

The donkey stood with black funeral bands on his lowered ears, and did not move. He stood right at the edge of the grave, and did not move, and each of us passed round him and did not dare push him out of the way.

I went back with Xaver Zlotogor and the donkey, taking the wide gravelled cemetery paths past distinguished tombs on the way. Here lie the dead of all faiths, not far away from each other; only the Jewish cemetery is separated from the rest by two hedges. Begging Jews stand there the whole day at this barrier and on the little avenues, like human cypress trees. They live on the charity of rich heirs, showering their words of blessing on every donor.

I couldn't but express my appreciation to Xaver Zlotogor, given how valiantly he had fought for the donkey. I didn't know the mesmerist at all yet; he didn't feature every day but only on Sundays and special occasions, and very often he was away as a 'freelance' on tour through small or smallish towns and giving performances.

He lives in the Savoy, on the third floor. He can afford it.

Xaver Zlotogor is a widely travelled man who knows both Western Europe and India. That is where he learnt his art, from fakirs, he tells us. He could well be as old as forty, but you really can't tell his age because he keeps such good control over his face and his movements.

There are times I think he must be tired; when we are walking together I think his knees are about to collapse under him, and because we have such a long way to go, and I am no longer so fresh myself, I want to suggest we sit down on a stone. But then to my astonishment Xaver Zlotogor leaps clear over the stone with his knees drawn right up high, like a boy of fourteen. At this moment he has a boyish face, an olive-green Jewish lad's face with impish eyes. A minute later he's wearing that tired expression again round the mouth, lower lip drooping, looking as if his chin is so heavy he has to rest it on his chest.

Xaver Zlotogor metamorphoses so quickly in these fleeting moments that he no longer appeals to me; I'm even driven to think the whole noble escapade with the donkey was just a mean comic act, and that the fellow wasn't always called Xaver Zlotogor; perhaps – the name suddenly springs into my mind – he was called Salomon Goldenberg when he was in his little Galician shtetl. Strange, how his bright idea of bringing the donkey to the cemetery had made me forget that he was a mesmerist, a shameless magician, a man who betrayed the Indian fakir's art for profit, and that his knowledge of the mysteries of an exotic world was limited to those trifling little magic tricks he'd learnt. And God let him live without punishing him!

'Herr Zlotogor,' I say, 'I'm afraid I have to leave you on your own; I have an important meeting.'

'With Herr Phoebus Böhlaug?' asks Zlotogor.

I was taken aback, and wanted to ask how on earth he knew, but I restrained myself and just said 'no' and then a quick 'Good evening', although dusk was still some way off and the sun had every intention of spending a good while yet in the sky.

I strode off quickly in the opposite direction, realised I was going towards the town, and heard Zlotogor shouting something after me, but did not turn round.

Bundles of mown hay gave off a strong smell, grunting came out of a pigsty, behind the huts stood some scattered shacks, their roofs of sheet-tin glowing like molten lead. I wanted to be alone till evening. Many thoughts, important and trivial, filled my mind, all of them invading my head like strange birds swooping in and flying away again.

I returned home late in the evening. The fields and paths lay in the dark, crickets chirped. Yellow lights burned in the village houses, bells chimed.

The hotel seemed empty. Santschin was no longer there. I had been in his room only twice, but still I felt as if I had lost a good, dear friend. What did I know about Santschin? At the theatre he was a clown, at home he was a sad, warm, down-to-earth fellow who suffocated in the steam from the laundry room; for years he'd breathed the fug of other people's dirty washing, if not in this Hotel Savoy in plenty of others. Every city in the world has its smaller or larger Savoys, and on the top floors of every one of them you'll have the Santschins living, and choking on the steam from other people's washing.

The Hotel Savoy was still full – of all 864 rooms there wasn't a single one empty; only one person was missing, only Vladimir Santschin.

I sat down below in the afternoon tea room. The doctor was smiling at me, as if to say: you see how right I was when I foretold Santschin's death? He smiled as if he were medical science itself, now celebrating his triumph. I drank a vodka, and looked at Ignatz – was this man Death personified, or was he just an old lift-boy? What was he gawping at, with those beer-tinted eyes of his?

Now I could feel hatred rising up inside me against the Hotel Savoy, this place where some lived while others died, where Ignatz impounded people's luggage and girls had to strip naked for manufacturers and estate agents. Ignatz was like a living ordinance of the house, Death and Lift-boy in one. I'm not going to be lured by Stasia into staying here, I think to myself.

My cash will last me three days; I have earned some money, with Glanz's help. Then, if I starve, they can bury me just like poor Santschin, far out on the other side of the graveyard, in a hole in the clay earth, all full of worms. The worms and snakes must be crawling all over Santschin's coffin already, and in another three days, or maybe ten at most, the wood'll be rotting, and along with it the old black suit which somebody gave him as a present and was already threadbare long ago.

Here stands Ignatz with his beer-yellow eyes and goes up and down in his lift, and he also brought Santschin down for the last time.

That night it was only with great reluctance that I was able to enter my room. I hated the bedside table, and the lamp, and the push-button, I made a loud noise knocking over a chair, and would gladly have ripped down the notice from Kalegyropoulos, which hung scornfully on the door, and I was fearful as I went to bed, and left the light on the whole night.

I saw Santschin in my dreams: I see him standing up in his muddy grave and shaving – I hand him a bucket of water, and he adds mud to it and coats his face with the mud as if it is shaving soap. 'I can do it,' he says, and: 'Stop looking at me!' and I stare in embarrassment at his coffin in the corner.

Then Santschin claps his hands together, and there's a loud burst of applause, the whole Hotel Savoy is applauding, Kanner and Neuner and Siegmund Fink and Frau Jetti Kupfer.

In front of me stands my uncle Phoebus Böhlaug, and he whispers to me, 'A fat lot you've achieved! You're not worth any more than your father, you good-for-nothing!'

XI

Just as I was leaving the hotel I bumped into young Böhlaug, wearing a pale felt hat. I have never in my life seen such a beautiful felt hat – a poetic creation, a hat of delicate, light, indefinable colour, scrupulously pinched and shaped in the middle. If I were wearing this hat myself I'd be loath to doff it, so I will forgive Alexander for failing to do so and merely touching it with his index finger, like an officer's salute in response to a military cook's greeting.

I am no less taken with young Alexander's canary yellow gloves – seeing this man, you could hardly doubt that he he'd come straight from Paris, and the most Parisian part of it at that.

'Good morning!' says he, with a sleepy smile. 'And how are things with Stasia – Frau Stasia?'

'I've no idea.'

'You've no idea? Don't make me laugh! Yesterday you were there with the lady following behind the coffin, you might have been her cousin.

'The donkey story is hilarious,' Alexander continues, removing one glove and waving it.

I remain silent.

'Now listen, cousin,' says young Alexander, 'I'd like to rent a place to stay the night – in the Hotel Savoy. Staying at home I don't feel free. Sometimes…'

Oh yes, of course, I understand – young Alexander puts his hand on my shoulder and pushes me into the hotel. I did not like this; I am superstitious and don't like returning to a hotel that I've barely left.

I have no reason not to follow Alexander, and I am curious to see what number room my cousin will get. I remember that the rooms on Stasia's right and left are occupied.

There is only one room left, the one where Santschin lived – his wife is already packing; she's supposed to be going to relatives in the country. Just for a moment I feel overjoyed that young Alexander from Paris will be living in Santschin's laundry fug – albeit only for a few hours or a couple of nights in the week.

'I'm going to make you a proposal,' he says. 'I'll rent you a room for yourself or give you your rent for two months – or if you want to leave this town I'll give you your fare to Vienna, Berlin, even Paris... and you make your room over to me. Fair deal?'

This solution had much to commend it, but still my cousin's offer took me by surprise. I now had everything I could have wanted – onward travel, money for the journey, and I'd now have no further need to count on Phoebus Böhlaug's good offices and could be a free agent.

All my entanglements were quickly resolving themselves. My wishes were being magnificently fulfilled. Just yesterday I would have sold a half of my soul for travel money, and now here was Alexander offering me freedom and money on a plate.

And yet I couldn't help feeling that Alexander Böhlaug had appeared on the scene too late. I should have thrown up my hands in joy and immediately said 'Done!' In fact I did nothing of the kind, but put on a pensive expression.

Alexander ordered schnapps after schnapps, but the more I drank the more dejected I became, and the thought of journeying on, and of freedom, entirely evaporated.

'You're not interested, dear cousin?' said Alexander – and, to show that it was all the same to him, he started telling me about the revolution in Berlin, which he happened to have seen at close quarters.

'You know, these bandits hang around for a couple of days and you can't be sure you'll escape with your life. I sit in the hotel all day long; down below they're getting the reinforced cellars ready for all eventualities, and they've also got some foreign diplomats living down there. I think to myself, farewell, lovely life! – I managed to dodge the war, and now the revolution has to get me! It was good luck for me that I had Vally there at the time. There was this little group of us young friends and we called her 'Vally the comforter', because she was our comforter in need, as it says in the Bible.'

'That's not in the Bible.'

'Well, who cares? You should have seen those ankles, my dear cousin – and her hair when she let it down, it reached all the way down to her bottom – those were crazy times. And what was it all for? You tell me, what did we need all that upheaval for?'

Alexander sat with legs splayed wide; so as not to spoil the creases, he stretched them far out in front of him and drummed his heels on the floor.

'So I'll have to search around for another room,' says Alexander, 'if you're not interested.' Then, 'I don't want to pressure you. Just think about it, dear Gabriel, till tomorrow – maybe…?'

Yes, of course – I will think about it. Right now I've been drinking schnapps, and on top of that this sudden offer has dazed me even more. I will think about it.

XII

We parted company at eleven in the morning, and I had plenty of time – a whole summer afternoon, an evening, a night.

And yet I could still have done with more time – a week, two weeks, even a month. Yes, I would happily have chosen a town like this for a holiday of decent length – it was a genuinely amusing place, was this town, with all sorts of wonderful people – it wasn't everywhere that you'd find people of this kind.

Here was this Hotel Savoy, a splendid establishment with its liveried porter and golden escutcheons, offering a lift and smart chambermaids in white starched nun's caps. Here was also the old lift-boy Ignatz and his contemptuous beer-coloured eyes, but what did I care about him so long as I could pay and didn't need to pawn any luggage? And then Kalegyropoulos, no doubt one of the nastiest you'd find – I didn't yet known him, nor did anyone else.

It would have been worth staying on here for Kalegyropoulos alone – I have always been attracted to mysteries, and a longer stay would definitely give me the opportunity to track down the elusive Kalegyropoulos.

Yes, no doubt about it, it was better to stay.

Here lived Abel Glanz the extraordinary prompter, and you could earn a little money from Kanner, and pick up some more in the muck on the streets in the Jewish quarter – it would be rather nice to make your entry into the west of Europe as a man of means. You could arrive here at the Hotel Savoy with nothing but a single shirt and leave as the proud owner of twenty trunks.

And you'd still be the same Gabriel Dan.

But don't I really want to go west? Have I not spent endless years in captivity? I can still see the yellow barrack buildings covering the white plain like a filthy scab, still taste the sweet final drag on a cigarette butt scavenged from somewhere, the years on the move, the bitterness of the highway – the awful frozen clods of mud in the fields bruising the soles of my feet.

What does Stasia mean to me? The world is full of girls, brown-haired, with large, intelligent grey eyes and dark eye-lashes, and delicate feet in grey stockings – lonelinesses can be joined, pains endured in company. Stasia can stay at the Varieté and be claimed by Parisian Alexander.

Off you go, Gabriel!

I happen to be roaming the streets once again as a farewell, looking at the grotesque architecture of the distorted gables and fragments of chimneys, shattered window panes pasted over with newspaper, impoverished shacks, the slaughterhouse on the edge of the town and factory chimneys in the distance, workers' huts, brown with white roofs and geranium pots in the windows.

The land all around has a melancholy beauty about it, a woman now fading, with autumn advancing everywhere although the chestnuts are still a deep green. Autumn should be spent somewhere else, in Vienna where you can view the Ringstrasse covered in golden leaves, houses like palaces, streets laid out straight and immaculate in readiness for distinguished visitors.

The wind blows over from the factory district smelling of pit coal, and there is a grey haze settling over the houses – everything resembles a railway station. I should be on my way. The whistle of a train sounds shrill – people are travelling out into the world.

I think of Bloomfield – so where exactly is he? They were expecting him long ago, the manufacturers are all excited, everything is lying ready prepared in the hotel, so where is Bloomfield?

Hirsch Fisch is longing to see him. Perhaps he'll now find a way out of his endless misery; after all, he's actually spoken with Bloomfield's father – he's called Blumenfeld, Jechiel Blumenfeld. I remember the lottery ticket I got from Hirsch Fisch, the numbers 5, 8 and 3 are a dead certainty, a triple win is in the bag! Just imagine, if my numbers came up, I'd be able to stay on in this fascinating town, take a bit more rest. I'm in no hurry. No mother, no wife or child. No one expecting me. No one yearning for me.

But I am yearning, to be sure – for Stasia, for instance. I would happily live with her for a year or two, or five. I'd love to go with her to Paris, if only I could get a triple win just in time before the government closes it down – I wouldn't have to sell my room on to Alexander, or go begging to my uncle Phoebus.

The draw is next Friday. There's a whole week to go. I can't keep Alexander waiting that long. I have to make up my mind by the morning.

I must say goodbye to Stasia.

She was dressed when I arrived, about to leave for her performance. In her hand she had a yellow rose, and she let me smell it.

'I've been getting lots of roses – from Alexander Böhlaug.'

Perhaps she's waiting for me to say: 'Send the flowers back.'

And perhaps I would actually have said it, if I hadn't come to say goodbye for ever.

So I merely said:

'Alexander Böhlaug is going to take my room. I'm leaving.' Stasia froze – on the second step – we'd just started going downstairs.

She might, perhaps, have asked me to stay – but I was not looking at her, and without pausing I went on doggedly down the steps as if I had no time to lose.

'So you're definitely going?' she said. 'Where to?'

'I'm not really sure!'

'It's a shame you don't want to stay…'

'Can't stay…'

That was all she said, and we went on together in silence to the Varieté. 'Are you coming for a farewell tea after the performance?' she asked.

If Stasia hadn't asked like this, but just invited me straight out – then I would have said yes.

'No.'

'Well then, have a good journey!'

It was a cool parting – but there again, there'd been nothing between us. I hadn't even sent flowers.

There were some chrysanthemums at the florist's in the Savoy – I bought them, and sent Ignatz with them to Stasia's room.

'You are leaving, Sir?' asked Ignatz.

'Yes.'

'Because, the fact is that there could be another room free for Herr Alexander Böhlaug – if Sir is leaving for that reason.'

'No, I am leaving anyway. Please bring me the bill tomorrow.'

'The flowers – for Stasia?' asked Ignatz, before I got out of the lift.

'For Fräulein Stasia!'

I slept the whole night without dreaming. Tomorrow, or the day after, I would be on my way – a train whistle came over, long and shrill – people were travelling out into the world – farewell, Hotel Savoy!

XIII

Young Alexander was a man of the world. He knew exactly how to clinch a deal. Blockhead though he was, he was still the son of old Phoebus Böhlaug.

He was there on the dot, in another smart suit. He spoke for an hour about everything under the sun, but not a word about the business in hand. He kept me waiting – young Alexander had plenty of time.

'In Paris I live with a Madame Bierbaum, a German lady. In Paris the Germans are the best housekeepers. Madame Bierbaum has two daughters, the older one's over fourteen, but even if she were thirteen – one doesn't worry too precisely about these things. Anyway – one day a cousin of Madame Bierbaum shows up – I'd been out on a trip with Jeanne – but she made me wait. I'll give you the short version – I come back after two days – I have the key with me – I arrive at night, tread softly so as not to wake anyone, on tiptoe as they say, don't turn on the lights, just take off my coat and boots and go over to the bed and put out my hand, and feel – now, what do you think? – yes, you've got it, the breasts of little Helene. She was using my room you see, because the cousin was there, or else

Madame Bierbaum had arranged it deliberately – well, in short, you can imagine what happened then.'

'I can imagine.'

Alexander embarks on a new story. This fellow had been through countless stories in his lousy twenty-two years. One story gives birth to the next one. I'm not listening any more.

Suddenly Stasia came into the tea room, looking for someone. We were alone in the room. Alexander sprang to his feet, ran over to her and kissed her hand, dragged her over to our table.

'We're neighbours now!' he began.

'Oh, I didn't know,' said Stasia.

'Yes, my dear cousin has been good enough to let me have his room.'

'That's by no means settled yet!' I said suddenly – I myself didn't know why. 'We haven't yet discussed it at all.'

'Is it to do with money?' asked Alexander.

'No,' I said very firmly. 'I'm not leaving at all. You can still have a room, though, Alexander – Ignatz has said so.'

'Ah, well, then everything's all right – and all three of us will be close neighbours,' said Alexander.

We talked on, about various things, then Ignatz came in; there were, he said, three rooms free – two would be taken tomorrow but one was definitely going to remain free, Room 606 – true, it was on the fourth floor, but it was a large room. No one wanted to take it because of its suggestive number – certainly not for ladies – but just for overnight stays, why not?

I left Stasia and young Alexander sitting there, and departed.

In the evening, in the lift, I was informed by Ignatz that Alexander had rented Room 606.

I went into my room as if it were a home I'd lost and found again.

Book Two

XIV

This is now my third day standing at the station and waiting for work. I could go to a factory if the workers weren't on strike right now. Philipp Neuner would be surprised to encounter one of the bar clientele among the workers. That kind of thing doesn't bother me, with so many years of hard grind behind me. No one needs workers, unless they have skills, and I've never learnt any skills. I can decline 'Kalegyropoulos' in Greek, and do a few other things like that. I can also shoot – I am a decent shot. Work in the fields gets you food and board, but no money – and I must have money.

You can earn money at the station. From time to time a foreigner turns up looking for a 'reliable person with knowledge of languages', so as not to be taken for a ride by cunning locals. Porters are also much in demand – there aren't that many of them round here. Apart from that I've no idea what I could do. You don't have to go far from the station to be in the world. From here you can see tracks leading out and away. People arrive, and travel on. Maybe a friend would come, I thought, or a comrade from the war?

And then one really did come, namely Zwonimir Pansin, a Croat, from the same company as me. He too arrives from Russia, and not even on foot, but by train, no less – so I can be certain that things are going well with Zwonimir, and he's going to help me.

We greet each other heartily, Zwonimir and I, two old war comrades.

Zwonimir was a revolutionary from birth. His military papers bear the initials P.S. – 'politically suspect' – and for that reason he never even got as far as corporal, although he wore a large medal for bravery. He was one of the first in our company to be awarded a decoration – Zwonimir wanted to turn it down, telling the captain to his face that he didn't want to be marked out, and regretted that things had come to this.

Well, the captain was very proud of his company – a good, if simple fellow, this captain – and had no wish to let the regimental colonel hear any hint of insubordination. Everything was arranged accordingly, and Zwonimir received his medal.

I remember the days – the regiment was off duty – when Zwonimir and I lay on the grass in the afternoon and looked over towards the canteen and saw the soldiers coming and going and standing around in groups.

'You must have got used to the fact by now,' said Zwonimir, 'that you'll never again be buying your condoms at a respectable shop, one of those sweet-smelling places with the shop girls perfumed like whores.'

'Yes,' I said.

And we talked about how this war would go on for all eternity, and we'd never get home again. Zwonimir still had a father and two young brothers.

'You'll be going the same way too,' said Zwonimir. 'Ten years from now there'll be no more fruit growing in any country anywhere, only in America.'

He loved America. When a billet was good, he'd say 'America!' If an emplacement was strongly constructed he'd say 'America!' Of a 'fine' lieutenant, again: 'America!' And because I shot well he'd dub my best shots: 'America!'

And anything enduring, anything permanent, would bring the word 'Go!' 'Go' was a command; when we were doing our physical exercises you'd hear the call: 'Go!' 'Heads down, now, Go!', 'Bend your necks, go!' And it would go on for ever.

When we were served up dried vegetables day after day, Zwonimir would say, 'Wire entanglement! Go!' Bombardments sometimes went on for weeks, and he'd say, 'Bombardment, go!' And because he took me for a thoroughly sound fellow, he'd say, 'Gabriel, go!'

We sat in the third-class waiting room with the noise of the drunks thundering around us; we spoke softly but still caught every word because we were listening with our hearts, not our ears. In this same waiting room someone before had spoken to me at the top of his voice, and I hadn't understood a word he'd said, the drunks were yelling so loudly.

These were Neuner's workers on strike, drinking away their strike money.

In the town, schnapps was prohibited; at the station you got your alcohol in coffee mugs. There were female workers there, young girls who were already quite drunk, but nothing could wholly destroy their freshness; the schnapps battled in vain against their good health. The young lads were getting into a fight over a girl and reaching for their knives, but they didn't kill each other. It was just a high-spirited group, not really angry; someone threw out a joke at the combatants, and they all made it up again.

And yet it was dangerous to sit here for long; you might suddenly receive a crack on the skull, or be shoved in the chest, or someone would come over and relieve you of your hat, or chuck you on the floor because he hadn't found a chair to sit on.

Zwonimir and I sat at the end, leaning against the wall so that we could watch over the whole room and quickly see anyone who approached us. But no one bothered us, and everyone immediately around us was friendly. Occasionally we were asked for a light, and once I dropped my matchbox on the floor and a young lad picked it up for me.

'Are you going to move on from here, Zwonimir?' I asked, and told him how things were with me.

Zwonimir was not intending to travel further. He wanted to stay here; he was enjoying the strike. 'I want to start a revolution here,' he said, as naturally as if he were saying 'I'm going to write a letter here.'

I learn that Zwonimir is an agitator, merely out of a love of unrest. He is impetuous fellow, honest and he believes in his revolution.

'You can help me with it,' he says.

'I cannot,' I say, and explain to Zwonimir that I am a loner and have no sense of community. 'I am an egoist,' I say, 'a real egoist.'

'An educated word,' Zwonimir reproaches me. 'All educated words are despicable. In ordinary language you could never say anything so repulsive.'

I have no answer for that.

I am on my own. My heart beats for me alone. The strikers are of no interest to me. I have nothing in common with any crowd, and nothing with individuals either. I am a cold creature. In the war I never felt really part of my company. We all lay in the same muck, all waiting for the same death. The difference was that I could only think of my own life and my own death. I walked over corpses, and sometimes it troubled me that I felt no pain.

Now the reprimand from Zwonimir leaves me no peace – I am forced to think about my coldness, my isolation.

'Every person lives in some kind of community,' says Zwonimir.

What community do I live in?

My community is the residents of the Hotel Savoy.

Young Alexander Böhlaug comes to mind – he also lives there, a 'close neighbour' to me. What did I have ever in common with young Alexander Böhlaug? Nothing, not with Böhlaug, but I did with the dead Santschin who was suffocated by the laundry steam, and with Stasia and the many others up on the fifth and sixth and seventh floors who live in fear of Kalegyropoulos's inspection rounds and have pawned their baggage, and are caged up here in this Hotel Savoy, on life sentence.

And not a hint of community with Kanner and Neuner and Anselm Schwadron, or Frau Kupfer and my uncle Phoebus Böhlaug and his son, young Alexander.

Yes, certainly, I live in a community all right, and its sadness is my sadness, its poverty is my poverty.

And now here I stand at the station and wait for money and find no work, and I still haven't paid for my room, and I don't even have a trunk to pawn with Ignatz.

It's a great piece of luck, this meeting with Zwonimir, a happy coincidence, the kind you only find in books.

Zwonimir still has money and courage. He wants to move in with me.

XV

We live together, in my room, Zwonimir sleeping on the sofa.

I don't offer him my bed. I am comfortable there, and I've gone without a bed for a long time. At home with my parents in the Leopldstadt there was sometimes little to eat, but there was always a soft bed. Whereas Zwonimir has been sleeping on hard benches all his life, 'on genuine oak!' he quips. He can't bear a warm bed, and any soft bedding gives him bad dreams.

He has a healthy constitution, goes to bed late, wakes with the first morning breeze. Peasant blood runs right through him; he doesn't have a watch but always knows exactly what time it is, can feel the rain and sunshine before it comes, smells far distant fires, and has premonitions and dreams.

One time he dreams his father has been buried; he gets up and sobs, and I don't know how to deal with this large weeping man. Another time he sees his cow dying and tells me about it and seems indifferent. We go around together all day long, Zwonimir gathering information from Neuner's workers about their conditions of work, and about the strike leaders, and he gives money to the children, and complains with the women and instructs them to go and get their men out of the waiting room. I marvel at Zwonimir's abilities: he hasn't yet mastered the local language, speaks with gestures and with his arms more than his mouth, yet everyone understands him perfectly; he speaks simply like the ordinary people, and swears in his mother tongue, but everyone round here understands a genuine profanity, whatever the language.

In the evening we go out into the fields, and there he sits on a rock and buries his face in his hands and sobs like a child.

'Why are you crying, Zwonimir?'

'Because of the cow,' says Zwonimir.

'But you've known about it all day. Why do you cry now?'

'I don't have any time during the day.'

Zwonimir says this completely seriously, and goes on weeping for a good quarter of an hour, then gets to his feet. He suddenly bursts out laughing, because he discovers a stone by the road side has been clothed like a scarecrow.

'These fellows are so lazy they can't even set up their scarecrows properly in the middle. Kerb stones aren't scarecrows! Show me a sparrow that's going to be scared of a kerb stone!'

'Zwonimir,' I plead, 'let's move on from here. Go home; your father's still alive, but he might die if you don't come and – well, then you won't have any more bad dreams. And I want to leave too.'

'Let's stay just for a bit,' says Zwonimir, and I know that nothing will move him.

He loves it at the Hotel Savoy. It's the first time Zwonimir has stayed in a big hotel. Nothing surprises him about Ignatz, the old lift-boy. I tell Zwonimir that in other hotels you have little milky-cheeked lads operating the lifts. Zwonimir says he thinks it's definitely more sensible for an 'American' thing like this to be entrusted to an experienced, older man. Besides, he finds them both weird – the lift and Ignatz. He prefers to take the stairs.

I point out the clocks to Zwonimir, and how they give different times.

Zwonimir says this is awkward, but still you must have variety! I show him the seventh floor, and the steam of the laundry room, and tell him all about Santschin and the donkey at the grave. He loves this story most of all. He doesn't feel sorry for Santschin, but he has a good laugh about the donkey later that night as he's getting undressed.

I also introduce him to Abel Glanz and Hirsch Fisch.

Zwonimir bought three lottery tickets from Fisch, and wanted to buy more and promised Fisch a third of the winnings. We went with Abel Glanz into the Jewish quarter; Abel did some good deals, and asked whether we had any German marks. Zwonimir had some German marks. 'Twelve and a quarter's the rate,' said Abel.

'Who's buying?' asked Zwonimir with surprising astuteness.

'Kanner!' said Glanz.

'Bring Kanner here!' says Zwonimir.

'What are you on about? Kanner's supposed to come to you?!' shouts the startled Glanz.

'Then you don't get my marks!' says Zwonimir.

Glanz needs to earn something, so runs to Kanner.

We wait. He comes after half an hour and summons us to the bar that evening.

In the evening we came to the bar, Zwonimir in a Russian military blouse and hobnails.

Zwonimir pinched Frau Jetti Kupfel on the upper arm and she let out a shrill squeal – she hadn't had a guest like this for a long time. Zwonimir had some schnapps mixed, clapped Ignatz on the shoulder, toppling the old lift-boy and bringing him to his knees. Zwonimir had a good laugh at the girls, loudly asked the names of the guests, addressed the manufacturer Neuner by name without using 'Herr', and asked Glanz, 'Where's that damned Kanner got to then?'

The gentlemen pulled wry faces and said nothing; Neuner didn't move either, but managed to appear pleased by whatever he heard, although he had done a year's service with the Prussian guard and had scars on his face.

Anselm Schwadron and Siegmund Fink conversed quietly, and when Kanner walked belatedly into the bar he wasn't welcomed with the greeting he'd expected and felt he'd deserved. He looked around, and picked Zwonimir out; when Glanz beckoned to him he came over to us and asked imposingly: 'Herr Pansin?'

'Yes Sir, Mister Kanner!' shouted Zwonimir in such a booming voice that Kanner recoiled half a pace.

'Twelve and three quarters!' Zwonimir thundered.

'Not so loud!' whispered Glanz.

But Zwonimir, in full view as everyone looked over at our table, pulled the money out of his wallet – he even had some Danish kroner, lord knows where from.

Kanner pocketed the money and did a quick calculation just to get things over with, and paid the rate – twelve and three quarters.

'My commission?' said Glanz.

'In schnapps!' said Zwonimir, and had five glasses brought for Glanz. Abel Glanz, out of fear, drank until he was reeling. It was an amusing evening. Zwonimir had wrecked the mood of the regulars. Ignatz was furious – his beery eyes glared. Undaunted, Zwonimir pretended Ignatz was his best friend, calling him by name – 'My dear Ignatz!' he'd say, and along would creep Ignatz, on his soft soles, an old tomcat.

Manufacturer Neuner had no interest in Tonka, and the naked girls came trustingly over to our table and pecked crumbs out of Zwonimir's hand. He fed them with pastry and crumbling cakes, and allowed them to sip from several glasses of schnapps.

They stood there in their white nakedness, like young swans.

At a late hour young Alexander Böhlaug arrived. He seemed downcast, though at the same time well turned out, and as he wanted to drown some sorrow or other Zwonimir was happy to oblige.

Zwonimir had drunk a lot, but despite this he was sober and ready for some fun, and he ribbed Alexander in a most amusing way.

'You've got points on your shoes!' said Zwonimir. 'Let's see how sharp they are! Where do you get your shoes polished? The latest thing in weaponry! Strike with French shoe spikes! – That tie of yours is nicer than my grandmother's headscarf, if ever I'm the son of Nikita, if ever my name is Zwonimir and I never slept with your wife.'

Young Alexander pretended he didn't hear. Grief was getting at him. He was sad.

'Personally I wouldn't have much time for that cousin of yours!' said Zwonimir.

'You don't get to choose your cousins', I said.

'No offence, Alexander!' Zwonimir bellowed, and stood up. He was huge, standing there like a wall in the little dark-red bar.

The next morning Zwonimir wakes early, and wakes me. He's already dressed. He tosses my coverlet onto the floor and forces me to get up and go out for a walk with him.

The larks are singing gloriously.

XVI

This was the day Kalegyropoulos was expected. Zwonimir was hurling the chairs around and bringing disorder to our room. He decided to lie in wait for Kalegyropoulos, to wait for him in our room. I waited for Kalegyropoulos downstairs in the tea-room, and Zwonimir stayed upstairs. This time I didn't see any excitement. Everyone had left the hotel; the upper three floors stood empty, and squalid domesticity was exposed to view.

Downstairs all was quiet. Ignatz was going up and down. After an hour Zwonimir came and said that the manager had gone down the corridor; Zwonimir had stood at the door, the manager had greeted him, but nowhere had there been a sign of any Kalegyropoulos. Zwonimir could forget these things easily, but the mystery of Kalegyropoulos would not let me rest.

Zwonimir makes his own independent excursions in the hotel, going into empty rooms and leaving notes with greetings, and after three days he knows everyone.

He knows Taddeus Montag, the cartoonist who paints signs and doesn't find much work because he makes a hash of every order he gets.

He knows the bookkeeper Katz, the actor Nawarski, the naked girls, and the two elderly maiden sisters, Helene and Irene Mongol. Zwonimir greets everyone loudly and cordially.

And Stasia, he knows her too, and he says to me:

'That little flotsam – she's in love with you!'

I feel pained – I know he means no harm, but the expression angers me.

I say: 'Stasia is a good girl.'

Zwonimir doesn't believe in good girls, and says he wouldn't mind sleeping with Stasia just to show me what a bad girl she is.

Zwonimir has already been down in the basement, the underground floor where the kitchen is. He knows the cook, a Swiss who's just called Meyer but can make fine puddings. Zwonimir gets free samples.

Zwonimir roughs Ignatz up – they're friendly blows, and Ignatz can't do anything about them anyway. I observe the way Ignatz braces himself whenever Zwonimir comes anywhere near him. It's a reflex, not real fear. Zwonimir is the largest and strongest man in the hotel, and he can comfortably carry Ignatz under his arm. He looks formidable, brutal, enjoys making a din, and when he's around everyone goes quiet and timid.

The old army doctor is fond of Zwonimir. The doctor happily stands him a schnapps or two in the afternoon.

'I know other doctors like you from the army,' says Zwonimir. 'You can strike living men dead, and you get paid a handsome salary for it. You can amputate people from the ground – you're a great surgeon. I wouldn't even want to trust you with the clap!'

But the doctor laughs. He's not offended.

'I could string you up!' says Zwonimir on one occasion, affectionately, and slaps him on the back. No one has ever slapped the doctor on the back.

'A marvellous hotel!' says Zwonimir, and has no sense of the mysteriousness of this building, where strangers, separated only by paper-thin walls and ceilings, live and eat and go hungry side by side. For him it is a matter of course that young girls pawn all their luggage and end up as the naked property of Madame Jetti Kupfer.

He's a healthy man. I envy him. Back in the Leopoldstadt you didn't see such healthy fellows around. He takes pleasure in life's vulgarities. He has no regard for women. He doesn't know any books. Never reads a newspaper. Has no idea what's happening in the world. But this is my faithful friend, who shares his money with me – and he would also share his life with me.

And I would do the same.

He has a good memory, and knows not only the names of people but also the numbers of their rooms. And when the room-service waiter says '403's been with 41', he knows immediately that the actor Nowakowski has been sleeping with Frau Goldenberg. And he knows a thing or two about Frau Goldenberg; she is the lady I met on the first day.

'Do you have enough money?' I ask.

But Zwonimir doesn't pay. He's already fallen victim to the Hotel Savoy.

I recall something poor Santschin once said. He had told me – this was just one day before he died – that all the people who lived here had become slaves of the Hotel Savoy. Nobody escaped from the Hotel Savoy. I warned Zwonimir, but he wouldn't believe me. He was healthy to the point of ungodliness, and he knew no power beyond his own.

'The Hotel Savoy has become *my* slave, brother,' he said.

Five days had already gone by since he arrived. On the sixth he made up his mind to work. 'We shouldn't be living like this,' he said.

'There's no work round here; let's move on,' I pleaded. But Zwonimir was going to find work right here for both of us.

And find work he did.

By the railway station, at the goods yard, there were heavy bales of hops. They had to be reloaded, and there were no railway labourers. There were a few drunken, idle fellows there, and the foreman could see clearly enough that with a workforce like this he'd be at it for months on end. Of all of Neuner's workers on strike, hardly ten presented themselves; then there were two Jewish fugitives from the Ukraine, and Zwonimir and myself. We got our food in the station kitchen, and had to be there at the ready at seven in the morning. Ignatz was taken aback to see me setting off in military shirt, mess kit and all, and returning home grimy from coal dust and work.

Zwonimir assumed command of us, the workers.

We work hard. They give us sharp pack-hooks and we plunge them into the hopsacks, which we roll onto small handcarts. When we've driven the hooks in, Zwonimir shouts his order: 'Hup!' Then we heave to, and – Hup! – we rest a moment – Hup! – and soon all the fat grey sacks were lying down inside. They looked like huge whales, and we're the harpooners. All around us are the whistlings of locomotives and flashing green and red signals, but we don't bother at all about them – we just work on. Hup! Hup! Zwonimir's voice drones, the men sweat, the two Ukrainian Jews aren't up to it; they're thin, puny little tradesmen.

I have pains in my muscles, trembling in my thighs. Just as I'm hurling out my pack-hook, I feel a heavy pressure in my right shoulder. The hook has to go right deep in, otherwise the sack tears and Zwonimir curses.

One time we got to the kitchen at twelve o'clock; it was a hot day, and we were tired. On our bench some guards sat chatting. They were talking about politics, and the minister and bonus pay. Zwonimir asked them to move along for us, but these officials felt they were important and wouldn't get up. Zwonimir turns over the long wooden table they're sitting at. The guards shout, and are about to strike him, but he sweeps their caps out through the open door. It looks as if he's decapitated them; with a single movement of his long arms he'd swept away half a dozen caps. The guards went off in pursuit of the caps, then came and stood there – without their eagles they looked quite pitiful, and after a few threats they withdrew.

We work hard, and we sweat. We can smell our sweat, our bodies crushed together, hands calloused, and we are united in our strength and in the pain we feel.

There are fourteen of us struggling with heavy hop-bales on their way to Germany – the people despatching and receiving them earn more out of them than all fourteen of us together.

That is what Zwonimir tells us every evening on our way home.

We don't know the person sending them; I merely see his name on the goods wagons: C. Merry, a charming name. Mr Merry lives in a nice house, like Phoebus Böhlaug, and his son studies in Paris and wears shiny shoes. 'Merry, don't excite yourself now!' his wife says to him.

What the receiver's name is I have no idea, but he'd have reason enough to be called Mr Jolly.

All fourteen of us were united – one single person.

We all turned up at the same time, all went to eat at the same time, all moved the same way, and the hop bales were common enemy to all of us. Mr Merry has welded and sweated us together, Merry along with Jolly. We see, with unease, that the bales are running out, that our work will soon come to an end, and our parting seems painful, as if we'll need to be forcibly severed from each other.

And I am not an egoist any more.

After three days our work was over. We were already free at four in the afternoon, but we stayed at the goods station watching our hop bales slowly rolling away towards Germany.

XVII

The homecomers' time has come round again.

They arrive in groups, many all at once. They are washed in like the shoals of fish you find in certain seasons. They are spewed westwards, these repatriated soldiers, by destiny; for two whole months there were none to be seen; then, for weeks on end, out they flood from Russia and Siberia and the borderlands.

The dust of years on the move lies on their boots, on their faces. Their clothes are in rags, their sticks are gnarled and worn. It's always the same way they come, and not on the trains but on foot. It must be years they've been wandering before they arrive here. They know about foreign countries and foreign ways of life – like me, they've sloughed off a good many lives themselves. They're vagrants, these people. Are they content to be on their way home, I wonder? Wouldn't they have remained more happily at home in the great wide world, rather than returning to that narrow little domesticity of wife and child and hearthside?

Perhaps that's not what they have in mind – going home. Westwards they are washed, like fish at certain seasons.

We stood, Zwonimir and I, at the edge of the town where the barrack huts are, for hours on end, searching for a familiar face among all these homecomers.

Many passed us, and we didn't recognise them, although we must certainly have shot next to them, and gone hungry with them. When you see so many faces you no longer know any one of them. They all look the same, like fish.

It is sad to think that a person goes past like that and I don't recognise him despite our having gone through an hour of death together. In life's most terrifying moment of all we were as one in our terror, and now we cannot even recognise one another. I remember feeling the same sadness when I saw a girl once – we met in a train, and I didn't know whether I had slept with her or simply had her mend my clothes.

Many of the homecomers wanted, like us, to stay in here in the town. The Hotel Savoy acquired new residents. Even Santschin's room was now occupied. Young Alexander had to sacrifice his little overnight nest, number 606, for three days when the manager declared that it was within his rights to let an unoccupied room.

As I was handing in my key I heard the dispute between Ignatz and Alexander.

Not having money for the Hotel Savoy, many resorted to the barracks.

It looked as though there was a new war about to break out. And so it all starts afresh once more: the barrack chimneys gushing smoke again, potato peelings lying in front of the doors, apple cores and rotten cherries, and washing strung up and fluttering on the line.

Things were becoming unsavoury in the town.

One could see returning veterans begging, and with no shame. They'd joined up as strong and proud men, and now they were unable to give up begging. Only a few looked for work. They stole from the peasants, rooted about in the ground for potatoes, clubbed chickens, wrung geese's necks, pillaged haystacks. They dragged all their plunder into the huts, and cooked there but didn't dig any latrines, and you could see them squatting down and relieving themselves at the side of the road.

The town had no drains, and stank anyway. On grey days in the narrow, uneven gutters by the edge of the wooden pavement you saw black and yellow muddy effluence, slime oozing from the factories, still warm and letting off steam. It was a God-accursed town. It stank as if it were on this place, not on Sodom and Gomorrah, that the Lord rained down His fire and brimstone.

God punished this town with industry. And industry is the harshest of God's punishments.

Here people were used to these periods of homecoming veterans, and no authorities bothered them. Perhaps the police were worried at having such numbers of unruly people around, and no one wanted any trouble. In any case Neuner's workers had now been on strike for four weeks; if it came to fighting, these new arrivals would be involved.

They came out of Russia, bringing with them the breath of the Great Revolution. It was as if the revolution had vomited them out into the West, like a crater spewing its lava.

The barrack huts had been empty for a long while. Now they suddenly became so full of life that you might think any moment they were about to spring into motion. In the night feeble tallow candles burned, but there was also a wild merriment all around. The young girls came to the soldiers, and they all drank schnapps, and danced, and spread syphilis.

My friend Zwonimir goes into the barracks; he loves excitement and disorder, and increasing it. He tells stories to the hungry about the rich, he rails against manufacturer Neuner, tells them all about the naked girls in the bar at the Hotel Savoy.

'Come on, you're exaggerating,' I say to Zwonimir.

'You have to, otherwise they never believe you!' he says.

He tells the saga of Santschin's death, as if he'd been there himself.

He has such a talent for describing things, his words breathe the spirit of real life.

The returning veterans listen, and then they sing songs, each one a song from his homeland, and they all sound the same. Czech songs, and German, Polish, Serbian songs, in all of them the same sadness, and all the voices equally raw and raucous and harsh. And despite that, the melodies sound so beautiful, as sometimes the tone of a beaten up old barrel-organ can be beautiful on March evenings, on Sundays at the beginning of Spring when the streets are deserted and have been swept clean by the great bells that ring out over the town in the morning.

The homecomers eat in the soup kitchen, and Zwonimir too. He says he likes the food there. For two nights we eat there together, and I see that Zwonimir is right.

'America!' says Zwonimir.

It was a thick bean soup. If you stuck your spoon in it stood up like a spade in the ground. It's a matter of taste; I love thick bean and potato soups.

No one ever opens the windows in the soup kitchen, and that's why the smell of old food lingers in the corners, and rises from the unwashed table surfaces when the steam of the new meal just cooked brings it to life again.

And the people sit packed closely together at the tables, with their elbows going to war although their souls are at peace with each other and their feelings are friendly.

People are not really bad so long as they have plenty of room. In large restaurants they nod cheerfully to each other, because they've found enough space. At Phoebus Böhlaug's place there's no fighting because people stay out of each other's way when it no longer suits them to be together. But when you have two sharing a narrow bed their legs fight and their hands tear the thin coverlet over them.

We took our place at twelve-thirty at the end of a long line of men. At the front of the line there was a policeman, waving a sabre in sheer boredom. We were let in twenty at a time, and we stood in pairs. Zwonimir and I were together.

Zwonimir was swearing because it was all going too slowly. He spoke to the policeman, who wasn't keen to answer – officials aren't supposed to talk.

71

Zwonimir called him 'du' and 'comrade', and once even declared that a policeman had no reason to be so mute.

'You're dumb as a fish, comrade!' said Zwonimir. 'And not even a live one – like one of those dead fish they fill with onions round here. Where I come from they only sign up chatty people as policemen, people like me.'

The women workers are alarmed by this kind of backchat, and are afraid of laughing.

The policeman sees that Zwonimir has the upper hand, and just twirls his moustache and says, 'Life's boring. There's nothing to talk about.'

'Come on, comrade, says Zwonimir, 'that's just because you went into the military police instead of joining up to fight. When you've been lying in the trenches the way we have, there's enough things to talk about for the rest of your life.'

At this point some of the soldiers have a good laugh. The policeman says, 'Our lives were in danger too.'

'Yes,' retorts Zwonimir, 'when you arrested a sparky deserter – sure, I can believe it, your life was in danger then all right!'

No doubt at all, the veterans loved my pal Zwonimir, and the policemen did not.

'You're a foreigner here,' they say to him, 'and you talk a bit too much.'

'I'm a soldier returning home, and am allowed to stop off here, my friend, because my government has an agreement with yours on precisely this matter. There's something you don't seem to understand: in my country we have enough of your kind, and if any of you lot here touches a hair of my head, my government's going to knock his head off for him. But it's clear you're not a student of politics – where I come from every policeman has to take an exam in the subject.'

These are persuasive arguments. The policemen keep quiet.

And Zwonimir was free to go on swearing day after day.

He swore when he had to wait too long, and again when

he was inside with his soup bowl in his hand. The soup was cold, or not salty enough, or too salty. His own discontentment spread to others, so they were all complaining, whether to themselves or openly, and the cooks behind the glass panes felt alarmed and added an extra spoonful on top of what they normally gave and what they'd been ordered to serve. Zwonimir increased the sense of unease.

The workers' women took the soup home in pots for the evening.

They could even have wrapped the soup in newspaper, the way they did their bread rolls, it was so thick and glutinous once you'd let it cool. All the same it was tasty and you took a long time eating it, and as they only let in twenty at a time the feeding lasted three hours.

The word was that the cooks were discontented and unwilling to work a whole day for negligible pay. By the second day there was no more to be seen of the women charity workers who were supposed to be overseeing things for nothing but the honour. Zwonimir had called one of them 'Auntie', and they were threatening to close the kitchen altogether.

'Just let them close the kitchen!' says Zwonimir. 'We'll have it open again in no time. Or we'll get ourselves invited to lunch by Mr Neuner. His soup's definitely better.'

'Yes, Neuner!' say the workers' women.

They were pale and wretched, and the pregnant ones dragged their poor expectant bodies about like an abominated burden.

'If you drag a bundle of sticks out of the woods, at least you know it'll keep your room warm,' says Zwonimir.

'Neuner would have paid bonuses for every child, and if they hadn't gone on strike in the first place we'd have got by somehow,' the women wailed.

'You'd never have got by,' said Zwonimir, 'there's no getting by if Neuner's going to make a profit.'

It was a brush-cleaning factory; they cleaned the dust and dirt from the pig bristles and made brooms out of them for further cleaning. The workers spent the whole day combing and carding the brushes, breathing in the dust and getting lung diseases and dying before they reached fifty.

There were all kinds of regulations on hygiene, the workers were supposed to be wearing masks, and the rooms in the workplace had to be so and so many metres high and wide, and the windows open. But a factory renovation would have cost Neuner much more than doubled child-allowances. So the army doctor was called in to see all the dying workers, and he testified on paper that they hadn't died of tuberculosis, or from blood-poisoning, but from heart problems. This was a heart-diseased race; all of Neuner's workers died 'as a result of cardiac failure'. The army doctor was a good sort, and he had to be in the Hotel Savoy every day drinking schnapps and dispensing wine for the likes of Santschin when it was already too late.

The workers' leaders also lived badly, but thought of themselves as the mayors of the factory, Neuner being the king. These days they were for ever searching for new ways of getting to Neuner. He would receive them with wine and bread and caviar, give them advance loans, console them by mentioning Bloomfield's name.

As far as the work was concerned, it was quite out of the hands of manufacturer Neuner.

Bloomfield, whose arm was long and reached right over the Pond, Bloomfield had some kind of involvement in each and every factory in his old town of origin. He only had to come over once a year, and everything would be sorted out, with no cost at all to Neuner.

Neuner waited for Bloomfield.

And so Bloomfield was awaited – and not only in the Hotel Savoy. Throughout the whole town people waited for

Bloomfield. He was awaited in the Jewish quarter, and people kept hold of their foreign exchange, and business was sluggish. They were longing for him in the upper floors of the hotel, Hirsch Fisch trembling in fear of some accident having befallen Bloomfield – there had already been some particularly handsome lottery tickets appearing in his dreams.

As it happened Hirsch Fisch had made an error over my ticket; the draw wasn't happening for another two weeks, as I found out in the community office.

Even in the soup kitchen everyone was talking about Bloomfield. When he came he granted every demand, and the earth took on a new complexion.

What did such demands mean to Bloomfield? He paid out as much in a single day on cigars alone.

They were waiting for Bloomfield everywhere. One of the orphanage chimneys has come tumbling down; nobody puts it right because Bloomfield gives some amount every year towards the orphanage. Sick Jews postpone going to the doctor because Bloomfield will soon be here to pay the bill. At the cemetery they've noticed some subsidence, two merchants have had fires and are standing out in the lane with their bundles of wares, with no thought of repairing their shops – what request would they then be able to put to Bloomfield? The whole world waits for Bloomfield, and people delay changing their bedding, taking loans on their houses, arranging weddings.

There's huge tension in the air. Abel Glanz tells me he has a chance of taking up a good job now. But he'd prefer to have a job with Bloomfield. Glanz has an uncle living in America; perhaps Bloomfield will give him his passage, without a job, and then he could get by and manage through his uncle's help.

Glanz's uncle sells lemonade on the street in New York.

Even Phoebus Böhlaug needs money to 'develop' his business. He's waiting for Bloomfield.

But Bloomfield does not come.

Every time the train comes in from Germany there are people standing at the station. Distinguished gentlemen arrive with brown and yellow travelling-rugs and big leather suitcases and mackintoshes and nicely rolled umbrellas in cases.

But Bloomfield does not come.

All the same, the people go the station every day.

Book Three

XVIII

Suddenly Bloomfield was there.

It's always the way with great events, with comets and revolutions and weddings of ruling princes. Great events tend to catch us unawares, and waiting for them only ever serves to delay them.

Bloomfield, Henry Bloomfield, arrived at the Hotel Savoy in the night – at 2.00 a.m.

At this hour there were no trains running – but Bloomfield, of course, was not coming by train – Bloomfield was hardly likely to rely on the train! He came from the border by car, his American saloon car, because he would not depend on the trains. He was like that, was Henry Bloomfield, the kind for whom the greatest certainty seemed doubtful, and if the rest of the world treated rail travel as something like a law of nature, along with the sun and the wind or the arrival of Spring, well, Bloomfield was the exception. He wouldn't even trust the timetables, no matter that they had state authority and bore an eagle and seals of several regional governments, and were the work of laborious computation.

Bloomfield came to the hotel at two o'clock, and Zwonimir and I were witnesses to the epiphany, as we were returning just at this moment from the barracks. Zwonimir had drunk a lot and kissed everyone in sight. Zwonimir could drink a good deal. Then as soon as he came outside he was sober and the night air removed any trace of intoxication – 'The wind blasts all the liquor out of my head,' says Zwonimir.

The town is quiet. A church clock strikes. A black cat darts across the pavement. You can hear the breathing of the people sleeping. All the windows of the hotel are dark, a night lamp lurks above the entrance, down the narrow lane the hotel casts a gloomy, gigantic figure.

Through the glass panes of the hotel door we can see the porter. He has taken off his braided cap – I observe for the first time that he does have a skull, and feel mildly surprised by the fact. The porter has a few little wisps of grey hair, growing round his bald head like a garland round a birthday platter. The porter has both his legs stretched out; he must be dreaming he's lying in bed.

The big clock in the porter's lodge says three minutes to two.

At this moment a shriek is carried in by the wind, and it seems as if the whole town is suddenly starting to scream.

Once, twice, comes this screaming, and then a third time.

Now a window is whisked open, and then another, two voices are speaking, a rumbling makes the wooden flooring shake under our feet, a white light fills the lane as if a fragment of the moon has tumbled into the narrow street.

The flash of white was from a light, a searchlight, a headlamp: the headlamp of Bloomfield's car.

And that was how Bloomfield arrived, like a night attack. The headlamp brings the war back to me, and I think of 'enemy aircraft'.

The car was a big one. The chauffeur was entirely done up in leather; he climbed out, looking like a creature from an alien world.

The car juddered a little while longer. It was spattered with mud from the main road; it was the size of a moderately large ship's cabin.

I felt just as I had done back on the battlefield, when a general turned up on inspection and it was my luck to be on company duty. I involuntarily stood up straight and braced myself and waited. A gentleman in a grey dustcoat got out, though I couldn't quite make out his features. Then came another man with his overcoat over his arm. This second gentleman was considerably smaller. He uttered a few words of English which I couldn't understand. But I did work out that the smaller one had to be Mr Bloomfield and the other man, his companion, was obeying some instruction.

And so Bloomfield was now with us.

'That's Bloomfield,' I say to Zwonimir.

Zwonimir wants to make sure of this there and then, so he walks straight up to the smaller man, who is waiting for his companion, and asks:

'Mister Bloomfield?'

Bloomfield just nods and takes a quick glance at this huge Zwonimir, who must seem like a looming church tower next to him.

Bloomfield then turns round again quickly to face the secretary.

The porter was now awake, and had put his cap back on. Ignatz hurried past us at this point.

Zwonimir didn't forget to deal him the usual blow.

The music had fallen silent in the bar. The small door was half open, and Neuner and Kanner were standing by it.

Frau Jetti Kupfer came out.

'Bloomfield is here!' she said.

'Yes, Bloomfield!' say I.

And Zwonimir shouted and danced on one leg like a madman.

'Bloomfield is here! He-he-here!'

'Quiet!' whispered Frau Jetti Kupfer, and put her fat hand over Zwonimir's mouth.

Bloomfield's secretary and Ignatz and the porter between them hauled two big trunks into the entrance hall.

Henry Bloomfield sat in the porter's leather armchair and lit up a cigarette.

Neuner came out. He was in a flush, the scars glowing on his face as if they'd been painted there in carmine.

Neuner went up to Bloomfield and Bloomfield remained seated.

'Good evening!' said Neuner.

'How's it going?' said Bloomfield, more a greeting than a question.

There was no real interest at all in the question.

Bloomfield – I could only see his profile – held out to Neuner a thin, childlike hand. It disappeared without trace into Neuner's mighty paw, like a little trinket into a king-sized packing trunk.

They spoke in German, but it seemed improper to listen.

Igantz arrived, talking away and with a board in his hand with a large black number 13 on it. He pinned it onto the middle of the door.

Zwominir dealt Ignatz a few blows on the shoulder. Ignatz did not flinch; he didn't feel anything at all.

Frau Kupfer came back to the bar.

I would happily have gone in there myself for half an hour or so, but it seemed risky to let Zwonimir go on drinking.

So we took the lift up on our own, for the first time minus Ignatz.

Hirsch Fisch arrived in his underwear. He wanted to come down to meet Bloomfield just as he was.

'You should get dressed, Herr Fisch!' I say.

'How's he looking? Has he already put on weight?' he asks.

'No! He's thin as ever.'

'My god, if old Bloomfield senior knew about this!' says Fisch and turns round again.

'If someone could kill Bloomfield!' said Zwonimir, when he was undressed and lying down.

But I don't answer him, because I know it's not him, just the alcohol speaking.

XIX

The next morning the Hotel Savoy feels different to me.

The excitement has got hold of me just like all the others; it has sharpened my eye to a thousand little changes, and I see them much enlarged, as if looking down a telescope. It is possible that the maids on the lower three floors are wearing the same caps as yesterday and the day before. But I have the impression that their caps and aprons are newly starched, as they would be before a visit from Kalegyropoulos. The room servants are wearing new green aprons. On the red stair carpet there isn't a single cigarette butt to be seen.

Everywhere is disconcertingly clean. You no longer feel at home here. You actually miss those familiar little corners of dust you'd got to know so well.

A spider's web in the corner of the tea lounge had been a reassuring familiarity – today there's a spider's web missing from that corner. It's true that you got your hand dirty from the banister rail, but now the surface is cleaner, more sterile than it's ever been, the rail might as well be made of soap.

I honestly think one could have eaten off the floor that one day after Bloomfield's arrival.

There's a smell of liquid floor-polish, as there was at home in the Leopoldstrasse the day before Easter.

The air has something festive about it. You expect bells to start ringing out any moment.

Any moment I might be given a present – it wouldn't seem at all out of place. That's what should happen on days like this.

And despite all this it was raining outside, a thin rain full of coal dust. A continuous rain, hanging over the world like a permanent curtain. People were bumping into each other with their umbrellas, and had their collars turned right up. It's only on rainy days like this you see the face of the town for what it really is. The rain is its uniform. This is a town of rain and despondency.

The wooden pavement boards start rotting, the slats squish under people's feet, like leaking wet soles.

The viscous yellow filth in the gutters goes liquid and runs slimily away.

There are a thousand grains of coal dust in every raindrop, and they remain stuck to the people's faces and clothes.

This rain could penetrate the thickest clothes. They're having a big clean-out in Heaven, and emptying their buckets down onto the earth.

On days like this you had to stay in the hotel, just sitting in the tea lounge and observing the people.

The first train to come from the West, at midday, brought three strangers from Germany.

They looked like triplets, and they got one room between them – number 16, I heard – they could all three have been got easily into one bed, like triplets in a cot.

All three had raincoats slipped over their summer coats, they were all equally small and had little protruding tummies of the same brand. All had diminutive black moustaches and small eyes and big check peaked caps, and umbrellas in cases. It was a miracle they didn't mix each other up themselves.

The next train, which came in at four in the afternoon, delivered one gentleman with a glass eye and a younger man, curly-haired and knock-kneed.

And then in the evening at nine o'clock, two more young gentlemen with pointed French shoes with thin soles. These were men of the most up-to-date style.

Rooms 17, 18, 19 and 20 on the upper ground floor were occupied.

And Henry Bloomfield – I met him at afternoon tea.

I owed this to Zwonimir, who was chatting with the army doctor. I was sitting there with them and reading a paper.

Bloomfield enters the tea lounge with his secretary, and the doctor greets him from our table. He's about to introduce Zwonimir when Bloomfield says, 'We've already met,' and offers his hand to both of us.

His little child's hand has a powerful grip. It is bony and cool.

The doctor talks in a loud voice and shows some interest in American affairs. Bloomfield speaks very little; his secretary answers every question. The secretary is a Jew from Prague, called Bondy.

He speaks politely and answers the stupidest questions from the army doctor. They discuss the prohibition in America. What can you do in a place like that?

'What do you do in America when you're feeling low – if there's no alcohol?' asks Zwonimir.

'You play the gramophone,' says Bondy. So this is Henry Bloomfield.

I've been imagining someone quite different. I was thinking Bloomfield must have the face, the suit, the gestures of a new American. I was thinking Henry Bloomfield would be ashamed of his name and his origins. No, not a bit. He talks openly about his father.

Bloomfield Senior used to say that drinking harms only the drunkard, and Henry Bloomfield, his son, still remembers his old Jewish father's wise sayings.

He has a small, canine face and big yellow horn spectacles. His grey eyes are small, but they don't dart around as small eyes tend to; these eyes are slow and searching.

Henry Bloomfield takes a good thorough look at everything, and his eyes learn the world thoroughly by heart.

His suit is not of the American cut, and his thin little frame has an old-fashioned elegance about it. A broad white ruff round his neck would have matched his face rather well.

Henry Bloomfield drinks his mocha very quickly and leaves the cup half full. He sips at it rapidly, like a thirsty bird.

He breaks a small cake in two, and leaves half on the plate. He has no time for food, neglects his body, concentrates on weightier matters.

His thoughts are on great undertakings, this Henry Bloomfield, son of old Blumenfeld.

Many people came by and greeted Bloomfield, and each time his secretary Bondy leapt to his feet, springing into the air as if on a rubber band, but Bloomfield stayed firmly seated. Apparently, in addition to his other duties, the secretary was Bloomfield's proxy for all courtesies.

To a few Bloomfield did extend his little hand, but most merely received a nod from him. Then he would insert his thumb into his waistcoat pocket and drum next to it with the other four fingers.

From time to time he gives a yawn, without people noticing – I only observed a wateriness in his eyes, and his glasses clouding over. He wipes them with a giant-sized handkerchief.

He seemed a very reasonable man, this little big Henry Bloomfield. The fact that he had to live in Room 13, of all numbers, was the only American thing about him. I can't quite believe his superstitiousness is sincere. It has struck me how quite often reasonable people deliberately adopt some minor eccentricity.

Zwonimir was remarkably quiet. He had never been so quiet before. I was afraid that he was mulling over the possibility of murdering Bloomfield.

Suddenly young Alexander turns up. He greets us with a deep bow, and generously deigns to doff his new felt hat. He smiles at me intimately, so as to make it obvious to everyone: these people sitting here are Alexander's friends.

Alexander walks up and down the room a few times, as if looking for someone.

In reality, though, he has no one to look for here.

'So America *is* after all an interesting country,' said the stupid army doctor, to fill the silence that had descended for a little while.

And off he went on his old jeremiad: 'Here in this town you just get countrified, your skull is sewn up tight and the brain shrivels away.'

'But not the throat,' I say.

Bloomfield glanced at me gratefully. Not a single mark in his face betrayed the hidden smile, just that his eyes took the trouble to look up over the edge of his spectacles, and took on a scornful expression.

'So you are foreigners here?' asked Bloomfield, looking at the two of us, Zwonimir and me.

It was the first question Bloomfield had put to anyone since he arrived.

'We're on our way home from the war,' I say, 'and just stopping off here for a break. We'll soon be moving on, my friend Zwonimir and I.'

'You'll have been on the road quite some time,' the courteous Bondy interposed.

This was a brilliant secretary – Bloomfield needed only give a cue, and Bondy was immediately translating Bloomfield's thoughts into speech.

'It's been six months,' I say, 'and who knows how much longer?'

'You had a rough time of it in captivity?'

'In the war it was worse,' says Zwonimir. None of us says much more today.

The three travellers from Germany come into the lounge, and Bloomfield and Bondy take their leave and go and sit at table with the triplets.

XX

The triplets' particular trade was in amusements and party goods – as I learned the following day from the room waiter. In fact they weren't real brothers, but their common interests had made them so.

Lots of people arrived from Berlin, Bloomfield's previous stop. They travelled here close after him.

Two days later Christopher Columbus came.

Christopher Columbus was Bloomfield's hairdresser. He belonged with Bloomfield's luggage, and was always following him later.

He is a talkative type, a German by descent. His father had been an admirer of the great Columbus, and had his son so named. But the son with the great name became a barber.

He is a man of sound business sense and good manners. He introduces himself to everyone as 'Christopher Columbus, Barber to Mister Bloomfield'. He speaks good German with a Rhineland accent.

Christopher Columbus is tall and slim, and has curly blond hair and good-natured eyes as if made of blue glass.

He is the one better-quality barber in this town and in the Hotel Savoy, and because he has no aversion to money and would otherwise get bored he decides to open a barber's shop; he seeks Bloomfield's help in getting permission.

There did happen to be a small room vacant next to the porter's lodge. Pieces of luggage were always lying in there, belonging to guests who were about to leave or had gone away for a few days and were coming back.

Ignatz informed me that Columbus would like to set up shop in this room.

And so he did – Columbus was a resourceful fellow. Being tall and thin, he seemed to fit well into any conceivable corner. He was generally destined to detect holes in things, and then fill them. That is no doubt how he came to be barber to Mister Bloomfield.

The people round here hardly appreciated that the barber was turning a famous name into a joke. Only Ignatz knew, and the army doctor and young Alexander.

Zwonimir asked me: 'Gabriel, you're an educated man; so did Columbus discover America or didn't he?'

'Yes.'

'And who was Alexander?' was the next question.

'Alexander was a Macedonian king and a great world conqueror.'

'Oh, I see.'

That evening we found ourselves together with Alexander in the tea lounge.

'What do you make of this barber fellow, Columbus?' Alexander laughed. 'To be called Alexander, of all things!'

Zwonimir glances at me quickly and says, 'For a barber to be called Christopher Columbus, that's surely not such a bad thing. Whereas you, you're called Alexander…!' That was a neat one, to which Alexander had no reply.

Sometimes I say, 'Zwonimir, let's be on our way.'

But Zwonimir doesn't want to leave right now. Bloomfield is here, and life is getting more interesting by the day. Every train brings more strangers from Berlin. Tradespeople, agents, layabouts. Bloomfield attracts all types. Barber Columbus shaves away for all he's worth. The luggage room looks very inviting with its two big wall mirrors and marble slab. Columbus is the deftest barber I've ever seen in my life. In five minutes the job's done. He uses the latest hair-cutting techniques, with the cut-throat razor. There's never any sound of scissors in his shop.

The devil alone knows where Zwonimir got the money for both of us. Our room account was already high enough. Zwonimir had no thought of paying it. He tucked his money under the pillow every night before going to sleep. He was afraid I might steal it.

We lived nearly as well as Bloomfield did, going to the soup kitchen when we felt like it. And if we didn't feel like it, we ate in the hotel. And our money never ran out.

One time I say to Zwonimir, 'I'll pack my things and go on on foot! If you don't like the idea, you can stay.'

And then Zwonimir cried – and the tears were genuine.

'Zwonmir,' I say, 'this is the last thing I'll say. Take a look at the calendar, today is Tuesday, we're leaving in two weeks from today.'

'Yes, absolutely,' says Zwonimir, and gives his solemn word, out aloud, although I haven't asked him to.

XXI

In the afternoon of the same day the secretary, Bondy, asked me to come to Bloomfield's table for a moment.

Bloomfield needed a second secretary for as long as he was staying here. It was necessary to divide the visitors into groups – the useful ones and the merely bothersome. And both lots had to be dealt with.

Did I happen to know of anyone, asked Bondy.

No, I didn't know anyone, apart from Glanz.

But at this suggestion Bloomfield's just waves his hand dismissively. Glanz had nothing to offer him, was what the gesture meant.

'You don't want to take the job yourself?' says Bloomfield. It was not a question. Bloomfield's tone never had anything of the interrogative; everything he said seemed to be addressed to himself, as if he were repeating things on which he had often pronounced already.

'Sounds interesting!' I say.

'In that case – could you, tomorrow in your room... which room is it?'

'703.'

'I'd like you to start tomorrow. You'll get a secretary.'

I take my leave, sensing how Bloomfield's eyes are following me.

'Zwonimir,' I say, 'now I'm Bloomfield's secretary.'

'America!' says Zwonimir.

My job was to listen to people, make an assessment of them and their proposals, and supply Bloomfield with a written report on those who called each day.

For each visitor I made notes on appearance, position, occupation, and proposed project, and then described all of these. I dictated to a girl who typed it up, and I took a lot of care over it.

After the first couple of days Bloomfield seemed satisfied with my work; he nodded at me very benevolently when we met in the afternoon.

It was such a long time since I'd last worked – I was happy. And it was the kind of work that suited me, because I didn't have to depend on anyone else and I was responsible for everything that I reported on. I took care not to report more than was necessary, but still on occasion I delivered a whole novel.

I worked from ten till four. Every day five or six visitors came, sometimes more.

I knew perfectly well what Bloomfield wanted of me. He wanted there to be a check on himself. He couldn't invariably rely on his own judgment – and anyway he didn't have time to reflect properly in each case – and also he wanted confirmation of his own perceptions.

Henry Bloomfield was a reasonable person. The amusements-triplets were called Nachmann, Zobel and Wolff; one visiting card accommodated all three names.

Nachmannzobelwolff had found out that in this part of Europe people hadn't yet come across these kinds of party goods and gadgets. They came with money, provided evidence for it, spoke very reasonably. This was the place where for years the spinning mill of the late Maiblum had stood empty. It could be repaired, said Wolff, at 'minimal cost'. Nachmann would stay here – it wasn't really so much Bloomfield's money they needed, but rather his name. The firm would be called Bloomfield & Co., and would supply this area, and also Russia, with party goods.

The triplets were going to manufacture fireworks, paper chains and streamers, jumping jacks and crackers.

I heard at the time that the idea had very much appealed to Bloomfield, and after two days I saw wooden scaffolding beginning to rise up round the Maiblum factory; before long the half-crumbling walls were bedecked with wood, like a monument in winter.

Nachmann, Zobel and Wolff stayed around for quite some time. They were to be seen, ever inseparable, prowling the streets of the town, all three coming into the bar and calling a girl over to the table. It was a cosy little domestic life they led.

People treat me with more respect than ever before in the Hotel Savoy. Ignatz lowers his inquisitorial beer-yellow eyes whenever he encounters me, in the lift or the bar. The porter greets me with a deep bow. The triplets doff their hats in perfect synchrony.

Gabriel, I tell myself, you arrive here with just one shirt and you depart as the proud owner of twenty trunks!

Secret doors open at my whim, men defer submissively to me. Wondrous things are revealed to me. And there I stand, ready to receive all the bounty that comes flooding towards me. People offer themselves to me, their lives lie unveiled before me. I can neither help them nor harm them – but they, overjoyed to find a captive ear to listen to them, pour out their sufferings and their secrets to me.

It's not going well for these people; their pain looms before them like a massive wall. They sit entangled in murky grey troubles and flutter around like captured butterflies. This one has no bread at all, that one has some but eats it with a bitter heart. The first craves food, the second freedom. Here someone flaps his arms, thinking they are wings and that just the next moment, or next month, or year, he will rise up and away on them, way above the depression of his world.

It was not going well for these people. They were preparing their own destiny, but thinking it came from God. They were trapped by traditions, their hearts hung by a thousand threads, and it was their own hands that spun those threads. On every path of their lives they faced the forbidding tables of the law, those of their god, of their police, their kings, of their own standing in life. Here they shall not go, there they shall not stay. And after a few decades of all the floundering and false starts and helplessness they died in their beds and bequeathed their misery to the next generation. I sat in the forecourt of the dear god Henry Bloomfield, registering the prayers and petitions of His little creatures. They came first to Bondy, and I received only those who could produce a chit from him. Bloomfield was going to stay for two or three weeks, and it took me just three days to see that he'd need to stay here for at least ten years.

I got to know little Isidor Schabel, who'd once been a notary in Romania but ceased to be so because of an embezzlement. He'd already been living in the Hotel Savoy for six years; he'd lived here during the war, along with the officers stationed here. He is sixty years old, he has a wife and children in Bucharest, and they're ashamed of him – they've no idea where he is. Now, he thinks, now might be the time to set to work and reinstate himself. Fifteen years have gone by since that unhappy story; surely it must now be time to return home, to see what his wife and children are up to, see if they are alive, see whether his son has become an officer despite his father's misfortune. He is a remarkable person – he wants to know his son's rank, and he has so many worries. He survives working as a back-street copyist. Every now and then a Jew comes to him to get an application written to the authorities – an exemption from death duties, for example.

His trunks were long ago all pawned to Ignatz, he lives on roasted potatoes at midday, but he wants to know whether his son is an officer.

He did go to Bloomfield once a year ago – but with no success.

He needs a tidy sum to re-establish himself. He remained doggedly convinced that right was on his side.

He was being devoured to the marrow with bitterness. Today he was still asking demurely, but tomorrow he'll be swearing, and in a year he'll be in the grip of madness.

And I know Taddeus Montag, Zwonimir's friend, the sign-painter who's really a cartoonist. He is my neighbour in room 705. I've been here for a few weeks now, and all the while Taddeus Montag was starving alongside me, and never uttered a word. People are mute, muter than fish; there was a time they'd cry out if something hurt them, but as time went on they got out of the habit of crying. Taddeus Montag is a sure candidate for death, thin, pale, tall, he creeps around softly, you don't hear his tread on the bare flagstones up on the sixth floor. True, the soles of his shoes are torn, but even the soft slippers of Hirsch Fisch can be heard on these floors. Taddeus Montag, though, has the noiseless phantom soles of a departed spirit. He comes in silence, stands like a mute at the door, and tears my heart with his dumbness.

He just can't help it, Taddeus Montag, not earning any money. He drew cartoons of the planet Mars, or the moon, or of long-dead Greek heroes. You could find Agamemnon there, in his pictures, cheating on Clytemnestra – out in the fields with a buxom young Trojan maiden. And on a hillock stood Clytemnestra observing her husband's shameful behaviour through giant opera-glasses.

I remember Taddeus Montag doing a crazy grotesque version of the whole history of the Pharaohs, right up to present times. He delivered these insane pictures in as matter-of-fact a way as if he were showing us trouser buttons for our selection. One time Taddeus Montag made a sign for a master joiner. In the middle he put a vast, oversized plane, and next to it on a wooden trestle table a man with a pince-nez sharpening a pencil on this monstrous implement.

What's more, he actually delivered the sign.

Fabulous liars appeared, such as the man with the glass eye who wanted to open a cinema. At the time the export of German films was very difficult, and Bloomfield knew it; he didn't want to get involved.

In this town there's nothing so lacking as a cinema. It is a grey town, with lots of rain and gloomy days, and the workers on strike. Time is something people do have. Half the town would sit all day, and half the night, in a cinema.

The man with the glass eye is called Erich Köhler. He is a minor theatre director from Munich. He was originally from Vienna, he tells me, but he can't fool me, knowing the Leopoldstadt as I do. Erich Köhler, without a shadow of doubt, comes from Czernowitz, and he didn't lose that eye in the war. It would have had to be a much bigger world war for that. He is an uneducated man, gets foreign words muddled up. He's a bad man – he doesn't lie for the fun of lying, but sells his soul for shabby profiteering.

'In Munich I opened the Picture House, with a statement to the press and all the authorities. It was the last year of the war, and if the revolution hadn't come – well, then you'd have a better idea who Erich Köhler is.'

And a mere quarter of an hour later he's telling us about his close friendships with Russian revolutionaries.

He was a one-off, was Erich Köhler!

The other gentleman, the young fellow with the French shoes, an Alsatian, was offering Gaumont films, and really did start up a cinema. Bloomfield had no great inclination to provide the people of his home town with entertainments, but the young Frenchman bought a dairy from Frankel, whose business had run aground, and printed posters and billed programmes for decades ahead.

No, getting money out of Bloomfield was no easy matter.

I was with Abel Glanz in the bar, and all the old crowd were there. Glanz told me in confidence – Glanz told everything in confidence – that Neuner had got nothing from Bloomfield, and that Bloomfield had absolutely no interest in doing any more business around these parts. In a single year his fortune went up tenfold in America – why should he have any interest in bad foreign currency?

Bloomfield had disappointed many people. They hadn't got rid of their foreign currency, and business was still on much the same track as if Bloomfield had never arrived from America. But I still couldn't understand why the manufacturers were now suddenly turning up with their wives, and with their daughters.

In fact around this time the company in the tea lounge was being quite transformed.

First of all, Kalegyropoulos has provided some music, a five-man band that plays waltzes as well as marches, all charged with emotion. Five Russian Jews play operetta every evening, and the lead violin sports curly hair for the ladies.

Ladies were never seen here before.

Now Manufacturer Neuner was there with wife and daughter, and there was Kanner, a widower with two daughters, and Siegmund Fink had a young wife, and then came my uncle Phoebus Böhlaug, along with his daughter.

Phoebus Böhlaug greets me with heartfelt reproaches – I should have been calling on him.

'I don't have any time now,' I say.

'You don't need money anymore,' answers Phoebus.

'You never gave me any in any…'

'Sorry, no offence!' chants my Uncle Phoebus.

XXII

I couldn't understand what Henry Bloomfield had really come for. Was it just to hear the music played? Or so that the ladies would appear?

One day Zlotogor, Xaver Zlotogor the Mesmerist materialised in the afternoon tea lounge. He was wearing his knavish young Jew's expression, going round between the tables greeting the ladies, while they nodded towards him amiably and asked him to join them.

He had to sit down at each table, and each time he sat for five minutes before standing up again and kissing the ladies' hands – twenty-five pairs of ladies' hands in one hour.

He came over to me too; Zwonimir was sitting there with me and asked him:

'Are you the fellow with the donkey?'

'Yes, said Zlotogor, slightly disconcerted – he was a taciturn person whose element was silence, and he disliked Zwonimir's loudness.

'Good joke!' Zwonimir goes on appreciatively, without seeing that his loud cheeriness is not welcomed.

Still, this wasn't enough to drive Xaver Zlotogor into retreat.

On the contrary, he now sat himself down and informed me that he'd had a good idea. This was not the right season for public mesmerism, so he thought he'd take advantage of the holiday season to do some private practice – in the hotel, in his large room on the third floor. He would receive ladies suffering from headaches.

'Splendid idea,' shouts Zwonimir.

'Herr Doctor!' shouts Zwonimir over to the army doctor, and Zlotogor, Mesmerist, sits there wanting to stick a knife into Zwonimir. But it would take more than magnetism to dent Zwonimir's strong nature.

The army doctor comes over.

'You're in for some competition,' says Zwonimir, and points to the mesmerist.

Xaver Zlotogor leapt up, hoping to stave off any further misfortune and silence Zwonimir's booming voice, and gave his own account of what he intended.

'Thank God for that,' says the army doctor, who doesn't care much for work. Now I can stop prescribing aspirin! I'll send you all my patients.

'I'm much obliged to you,' says Zlotogor, and bows respect-fully.

And indeed the next day a few ladies did come, and they sent messages up Zlotogor. No one was bold enough to enter the hotel, but Zlotogor wasn't too particular, and was happy to go to houses and mesmerise them at home.

'It's remarkable,' I say to Zwonimir, 'have you seen how people change because my boss Bloomfield is around? Every-one's suddenly having business ideas, in the hotel here, and in the town. Everyone wants to make money.'

'I've also had an idea,' said Zwonimir.

'What?'

'To finish Bloomfield off.'

'What for?'

'Just for the hell of it – it's not a business idea, and there's no particular point in it.'

'Incidentally, do you know what Bloomfield's here for?'

'To do some business.'

'No, Bloomfield couldn't give a damn about business round here. I'd give anything to know what he's really here for. Maybe he's in love with a woman. But he could always take her back over there with him. A woman's not like a house. But perhaps she's already married – in that case she'll be even harder to take away than a house. I really can't believe Bloomfield comes all this way just to repair the late Maiblum's old factory. He's not interested in streamers and crackers. He's got enough money to supply half of America with party goods. Do you really think he's come over to finance a cinema in his old town? He doesn't even give any money to Neuner, and his workers are in the fifth week of a strike!'

'Why doesn't he give away any money?' says Zwonimir.

'Ask *him*.'

'I'm not going to ask him. It's nothing to do with me. That's mean.'

It seemed to me that Neuner was just talking his way out of things with Bloomfield, and he no longer had any interest in factories. Times were bad, money had lost its value. According to Abel Glanz, Neuner preferred to gamble on the Zurich Stock Exchange, and was dealing in foreign exchange. Telegrams were coming for him every day – from Vienna, Berlin, London. People were cabling the rates to him, and he was sending orders back; what interest could he have in the factory?

There was no point trying to explain these complicated things to Zwonimir, nor did he wish to understand them, because he felt it cost him mental effort; he was a peasant, and he went every day to the barrack huts, not for the sake of the homecomers but because the barracks were right out next to the countryside, and Zwonimir's soul yearned for the sheaves and scythes and scarecrows of his homeland fields.

Every day he brings me news of the wheat, tucks away blue cornflowers in his pocket. He curses because the peasants round here have no idea how to treat the soil properly – they're perfectly happy to let their cows roam, as animals will. So they roam in among the crops, and it's almost impossible to coax them out.

And the scarecrows and the kerb stones, he can't forget those either.

He comes home in the evening, Zwonimir Pansin, the peasant, and with him he brings an overwhelming longing, a hidden yearning for home. He awakens a yearning in me too, and although he pines for the fields, and I for streets, his sickness infects me. It's the way it is with songs from your native land: one person only has to sing a few notes of a song from his homeland, and another person will start one from his own land, and soon the different tunes blend together in one, and all of them are merely the different instruments of a single band.

Our homesickness is born out in the open, and grows and grows if there are no walls to confine it.

On Sunday morning I walk out amongst the fields, where the grain stands high as a man and the wind hovers in the white clouds. I walk slowly, over towards the cemetery; I want to find Santschin's grave. I find it after long searching. In this short time so many had died, and all were obviously poor, for they lay close to the Santschin grave. Things are bad for the poor at this time, and death hands them on to the worms in the soil.

I found Santschin's grave, and I thought to myself – now I should say farewell to his last earthly remains. He died too early, did our good clown. He should have lived to meet with Henry Bloomfield; might he even perhaps have won that journey to the south? I climb over the low hedge that closes off the Jewish graveyard, and I notice some commotion among the poor Jews, the beggars who live off the charity of wealthy heirs. They no longer stand singly like solitary weeping willows at the start of a lane, but in a group, and they are talking fast and loud. I hear the name Bloomfield and listen in for a little, and learn that they're waiting for Bloomfield.

This seemed to me to be very important. I ask the beggars, and they tell me this is the anniversary of the death of old Blumenfeld, and that is why Henry, his son, comes here.

The beggars know all the rich people's anniversaries, and what's more it's *only* they who know what Henry Bloomfield is here for. It's the beggars who know, not the big factory owners.

Henry Bloomfield came on a visit to his departed father Jechiel Blumenfeld. He came to thank his father for all those many millions, for the talent, for the life, for everything, that he had inherited. Henry Bloomfield didn't come to build a cinema or a factory for party wares. All the people think it's to do with money or factories that he comes.

Only the beggars know the purpose of Bloomfield's journey.

It was a homecoming.

I waited for Henry Bloomfield. He came alone. He had come to the cemetery on foot, His Majesty Bloomfield. I saw him there before the grave of old Blumenfeld. I saw him stand and weep. He took off his glasses, and the tears ran down his thin cheeks, and he wiped them with his little child's hands. Then he took out a bundle of banknotes, the beggars fell all around him like a swarm of flies, he disappeared in the midst of all the dark shapes to whom he gave money, redeeming his soul from the sin of wealth.

I did not want to be found lurking there unnoticed, and I went up to Bloomfield and greeted him. He was not in the least surprised to see me there – what would ever surprise Henry Bloomfield? He gave me his hand, and asked me to accompany him back to town.

'I come here every year,' said Bloomfield, 'and visit my father. I cannot forget the town either. I am an Eastern Jew, and for us people home is wherever our dead lie. If my father had died in America, I could feel quite at home in America. My son will be a real American, because that's where I'll be buried.'

'I understand, Mister Bloomfield.' – I am moved, and I speak as if to an old friend.

'Life hangs so visibly close together with death, and the living with their dead, there is no end there, no real break – always continuity and succession.'

'This is the land of the top-class scroungers,' says Bloomfield, recovering his humour – he is a practical, realistic man and forgets himself only once in the year.

I accompany him back to town, the people greet us, and I feel some return of pleasure: my uncle Phoebus Böhlaug passes and gets in his bow of greeting first, a very deep one, and I give him a condescending smile, as if I were the uncle.

XXIII

I understood Henry Bloomfield.

He was homesick, like me and Zwonimir.

People continued to come from Berlin and other cities. They were loud creatures, shouting and lying to drown out their guilty consciences. Braggarts, impostors, all of them from the film world with more than enough to tell about the world, but their goggle-eyed view of the world saw the world as God's commercial disaster; they wanted to compete with him, and start up businesses on an equally grand level.

They lived on the lower three floors and went to Zlotogor to have their headaches cured.

Many came with their wives and mistresses, and this kept Zlotogor really busy for the first time.

Much was changing in the Hotel Savoy.

There were ladies' evenings and gentlemen's evenings and dance groups, and all the gentlemen came rushing into the bar at midnight and pinched the naked girls and Frau Jetti Kupfer.

Up above us young Alexander walked around in his tails and patent leather, as did Xaver Zlotogor in a coat tightly buttoned to the collar, acting enigmatically with that naughty youngster's expression on his face.

Bloomfield came, and Bondy. Bondy spoke, but it was Henry Bloomfield that the ladies looked at, and because he said nothing it looked as if they were listening in to his silence, as if they had the ability to hear what he was thinking, and what he was hiding.

I was also visited by the people from the upper floors, and there was no end to it. I saw how none of them really lived voluntarily in the Hotel Savoy. Every one of them was oppressed by some misfortune, and for every one the Hotel Savoy was itself the misfortune, and he could no longer tell the one misfortune from the other.

It was through this hotel that every mishap struck these people, and they believed that their misfortune was called 'Savoy'.

There was no end to it. Santschin's widow came too; she now lived with her brother-in-law in the country, and had to work hard in the house. She had heard about Bloomfield's arrival, and that he helped everybody.

I do not know if Santschin's widow had any success.

I do not know how many people Bloomfield actually helped.

The police officer suddenly showed up, the same one whose whole family sat night after night in the Varieté theatre.

He was a young, stupid type with epaulettes, sabre at his side, and there was nothing special about him. He'd inherited room 80 from his predecessor; all the police officers stationed here had room 80, without charge. For a week the officer had been wearing a new dark-blue cloth uniform with a decoration on the breast. I think his promotions took him as far as First Lieutenant. He strutted ceremoniously, his sabre quite often getting in between his legs while his right hand was occupied flourishing his yellow suede gloves. He came into the bar and drank at everyone's table, at everyone's expense, and finally came to rest at young Alexander's table.

The two of them got on splendidly.

The police officer has a close-trimmed moustache, a short little stubby nose, and big red ears mounted on a small shaved skull. His hair grew well down his forehead in a pointed triangle above the nose, and he had to perch his service cap right down over his eyes to avoid people seeing this absurd hair-style.

I admit ignorance when it comes to what a police officer has to do, but I do know that he has very little work. Our officer got up at ten, took luncheon at midday, then read the newspapers. A taxing routine, for which he took off his sabre while reading the papers – wearing his civilian hat, as it were.

In the evenings he cut a dashing figure on the dance floor – where he was much in demand. He pollinated himself with lily-of-the-valley, smelt like a flower-stall, and danced in tight trousers anchored to his boots with rubber straps. The trousers had a thin red stripe at the seam, which glowed very brightly and very lustily. His massive ears blazed like flames of deep purple, and he used a delicate laced handkerchief to dab the beads of perspiration from his nose.

The police officer was called Jan Mrock. He was politeness itself, very agreeable, always smiling.

That smile was his salvation – a gift from some kindly guardian angel.

When I looked at him like this, with his rosy skin and innocent face, I could tell that he hadn't changed in the slightest since the age of seven. He looked just like a schoolboy. Twenty years of war and affliction left him untouched.

Once he came into the bar with Stasia.

It is two weeks since I last saw her. She is brown and fresh, smiling, her eyes big and grey.

'You're still here?' says Stasia and blushes; it's a sham, she knows perfectly well that I haven't gone away.

'Are you disappointed?'

'You've been neglecting our friendship!'

I'm not one to neglect friendship. It's Stasia who deserves that reproach.

Two weeks lie between the two of us. Two hundred years could not work more devastation. I have waited trembling for her outside the Varieté, hunched into the shadow of a wall. We have drunk tea together, and a gentle warmth enveloped us both. She was my first encounter with love in the Hotel Savoy, and both of us disliked young Alexander.

I have peeped through her keyhole and seen her pacing up and down in her bathrobe, learning her French vocabulary. That's where she wants to go, to Paris.

I would have travelled with her to Paris any time. I would happily have stayed with her, a year, or two years, or ten.

A huge weight of loneliness has accumulated in me, six years of immense loneliness.

I search for reasons why I have drifted so far from her, and I cannot find any. I look for reproaches – but what could I have reproached her with? She accepted flowers from Alexander without sending them back. It's stupid to send flowers back. I may be jealous? When I compare myself with Alexander Böhlaug, there's pretty well everything to be said in my favour.

And yet that's what I am – jealous.

Conquest is not my way, nor is adoration. If something presents itself to me I take it and feel grateful for it. But Stasia offered me nothing. She wanted to be besieged.

I didn't see it at the time. I'd been alone so long, without women around me. I didn't see why it was that girls act so indirectly, and have such patience, and remain so proud. Stasia couldn't have known that I would never have accepted her triumphantly, but would have done so humbly and thankfully. Today I understand that it is part of women's nature to hesitate, and their little deceits are to be forgiven, and amount to nothing.

I cared too much about the Hotel Savoy and the people in it, and about the fate of others, and too little about my own fate. Here before me was a beautiful woman just waiting for a single word, and I, like a stubborn schoolboy, failed to say the word.

And I was stubborn. To me it was as if my long loneliness were Stasia's fault, but in fact she had no inkling of it. I blamed her for not having a sixth sense.

Now I realise that women do sense everything that's going on inside us, and yet are waiting to hear the words.

God made that timidity part of the woman's soul.

Her presence enchanted me. Why didn't *she* come to *me*? Why let herself be escorted by the police officer? Why ask if I'm still here? Why didn't she say: 'Thank God you're here!'

But there again, if you are a poor girl, perhaps you don't say to a poor man, 'Thank God you're here!' Perhaps the moment has passed for you to love a poor Gabriel Dan, who doesn't even have a trunk to his name, let alone a house. Perhaps the time has now come for girls to love an Alexander Böhlaug.

Today I know that it was sheer chance she was being escorted by the police officer, and her question was, in fact, a declaration. But at that time I was lonely and embittered, and I behaved as if I were the girl, and Stasia the man.

She grows even prouder and cooler, and I feel the distance increasing between us, and how we are becoming more and more like strangers to one other.

'I am definitely on my way in ten days,' I say.

'If you're going to Paris, send me a card.'

'Glad to!'

Stasia could have said, 'I'd like to go to Paris with you.'

Instead of which, she asks me to send a card.

'I'll send you one of the Eiffel Tower.'

'Whatever you like!' said Stasia, and she's not thinking of the postcard, but the two of us.

That is our last conversation. I know it is our last conversation. Gabriel Dan, there's nothing you can expect from girls; you are a poor man, Gabriel Dan!

Next morning I see Stasia going downstairs on young Alexander's arm. The two of them smile at me – I am having breakfast downstairs. And at that moment I know that Stasia has done something really stupid.

I understand.

Women commit their stupidities not because of recklessness or thoughtlessness, as we men do, but only when they are very unhappy.

Book Four

XXIV

I love the yard my window looks out on. It reminds me of that first day in the hotel, the day I arrived. I still see children playing, hear a dog barking, enjoy the colourful flag-like washing fluttering on the lines.

My room has seemed restless ever since I first received Bloomfield's visitors. There is a restlessness all over the hotel, in the corridor, in the afternoon tea room, and the town itself is oppressed by an unrest that wafts around with the coal dust.

When I look out of the window I see one fragment of happily rescued calm. The cocks are crowing. Only the cocks.

The Hotel Savoy had one other light well, a narrow one that looked like a shaft made for suicides. It was used for beating out mats and shaking out the dust and cigarette ends and all the detritus of relentless life.

But my back yard felt as if it did not belong to the Hotel Savoy at all. It lay hidden behind the huge walls. I would like to know what has happened to that courtyard.

It is like that with Bloomfield too. When I think of him, I long to know whether he is still wearing that pair of yellow horn-rims. And I'd also love to hear about Christopher Columbus the barber. What gap, what opening in life has he found to fill now?

Great events have been known to have their origins in barber's shops. There, in the little saloon of barber Christopher Columbus in the Hotel Savoy, it once happened that one of Neuner's workers on strike started a spat.

Business was going along well. All kind of news could be heard every morning at Columbus's shop. The great and good of the town, the police officer no less, all the newcomers, and the majority of the local guests of the hotel, used him as their barber. And then one day a labourer came into the shop slightly drunk, and met all the distasteful glances he got with barefaced indifference.

He had his shave, and failed to pay. Christopher Columbus, being a generous sort of fellow, would have let him off. But Ignatz threatened to call the police. Whereupon the labourer lashed out at him. The police arrested him.

That afternoon the man's comrades moved in on the hotel and yelled out their disapproval, then went on to the prison.

And during the night they marched through the terrified streets, chanting songs as they went.

The newspaper carried a report blazing out in large print from the middle of the front page. A few miles ahead the workers from a large textile factory had joined the strike. The paper called on the military, the police, on the authorities, on God himself.

The writer declared that all this devilry started with the home-comers, who had come and spread the 'bacillus of Revolution through our healthy land'. This writer, a miserable enough specimen, was evidently squirting ink against avalanches, building paper dams against tidal waves.

XXV

It has now been raining for a week in the town. The evenings are clear and cool, but during the day it rains.

It fits well with the rain that these days the flood of home-coming veterans has started rolling in again, and with a new frenzy.

Through the thin, obliquely falling rain they make their way; Russia, the great Russia, spills them out. There's no end to them. They have all come by the same route, all in their grey clothing, the dust of all those years of wandering on their feet and faces. It is as if they and the rain belong to one another. Both are grey alike, and both unchanging.

They flood forth in their greyness, unending grey over the greyness of this town. Their tin vessels rattle like the rain in the gutters. A great homesickness radiates from these people, driven on by yearning, by yearning and an overpowering memory of home.

On their journey they hunger, and they steal or beg, not caring which. They kill geese and chickens and calves, now that there is peace in the world – but that only means you no longer need to kill people.

Geese, chickens, calves, though, have nothing to do with peace. We stand there, Zwonimir and I, at the edge of the town where the barracks are, and watch for familiar faces. All of them strangers, yet all familiar. One looks like the man who used to march next to me, and another the one who taught me my exercises.

We stand at the side and watch them, but it feels just as if we were marching with them. We are like them, we too spilled out from Russia, and we are all on our way home.

One comes with a dog; he's carrying the animal in his arms, his metal bowl clattering against his hip with each step. I know he'll get the dog home; his home is down south, in Zagreb or Sarajevo, and he'll faithfully bring the dog home to his little house there. His wife sleeps with another man; they all believe him to be dead, and his children won't recognise him any more – he's become a different person now, and only the dog knows him, just a dog, a homeless dog.

These homecomers are my brothers, and they're hungry. They were never my brothers before. Neither out at the front when, driven by some incomprehensible purpose, we slaughtered strangers, nor back at our base where we all followed the order of some brutish fellow and flexed our legs and arms in time together. But today I am no longer alone in the world; today I am a part of the homecomers.

They swept slowly through the town in groups of five or six, and scattered just before the barracks. They sang songs of houses and farmyards in broken, rusty voices, and still the songs were beautiful, as sometimes on March evenings the sound of a leaky old barrel organ can be beautiful.

They ate in the soup kitchen. The portions got steadily smaller, and their hunger greater.

The striking workers sat drinking away their strike money in the waiting rooms of the station, while their wives and children went hungry.

In the bar, manufacturer Neuner groped at the breasts of naked girls, and the more distinguished ladies of the town had their headaches mesmerized away by Xaver Zlotogor. It was not in Xaver Zlotogor's powers to mesmerize away the hunger of the poorer women.

His art was only good for minor conditions. Hunger he could not treat, nor unhappiness. Manufacturer Neuner would not listen to Kanner's advice, and laid all the blame on Bloomfield.

But what did Bloomfield have to do with any of it, with the place itself, or its hunger, or any of its circumstances? His dead father Jechiel Blumenfeld was not starving, and it was for him that Henry Bloomfield had come here.

The town got its cinema, and a factory for party goods – and what was that supposed to mean to the workers' women? The party goods were for the well-to-do. What use were toys to a worker? Crackers and jumping jacks and a cinema might help them forget Neuner, but not their hunger.

XXVI

Zwonimir once said, 'The Revolution's arrived.'

Sitting there in the barracks and talking to the homecomers – the oblique rain falling outside, unendingly – we feel the revolution. It is coming from the east, and no newspaper, no army is going to stop it.

'The Hotel Savoy,' says Zwonimir to the homecomers, 'is a rich palace, and it's also a prison. Downstairs you've got the rich living in their lovely big rooms, Manufacturer Neuner's friends, and upstairs are the poor wretches who can't pay for their rooms and have to pawn their stuff to Ignatz. And the owner of the hotel – he's a Greek – no one knows him, not even the two of us, and let's face it, we're pretty smart.

'It's a good many years since any of us were lying in such nice soft beds like those ladies and gentlemen on the Parterre of the Hotel Savoy.

'It's a good long time since any of us were seeing such lovely naked girls as the gentlemen get to see down in the bar of the Hotel Savoy. This town is a poor people's grave. Manufacturer Neuner's workforce gulping down the dust from those brushes, and all dying by the time they get to fifty.'

'Shame!' shout the homecomers.

The worker who beat up Ignatz wasn't let out of prison.

Every day the workers gather in front of the Hotel Savoy and the prison.

Every day the papers blare out reports of strikes in the textile industry.

I can smell the revolution. The banks – or so you hear at Christopher Columbus's – are packing up their safe deposits and sending them to other towns.

'They're supposed to be recruiting extra police,' Abel Glanz informs us.

'They're about to intern the homecomers,' Hirsch Fisch tells us.

'I'm off to Paris,' says young Alexander.

Not alone but with Stasia, I thought to myself.

'We can't even get out now,' moans Phoebus Böhlaug.

'Typhoid has broken out,' the army doctor informs us in the tea lounge that afternoon.

'How do you protect yourself against typhoid?' asks Kanner's younger daughter.

'Death will come for all of us!' declares the army doctor, and Miss Kanner goes pale.

But for the time being Death only calls for one or two of the women workers. The children fall ill and are taken to the hospital.

They close the soup kitchen to reduce the risk of infection. No more soup for the hungry now.

The homecomers couldn't be kept in the barracks any more. There were too many of them.

There were whole hordes of them.

According to the police officer, they've applied for reinforcements. The police officer didn't seem greatly excited. He carries a service revolver, and gets up at nine now rather than ten. He flourishes his suede gloves; there might as well be no typhoid.

The sickness claimed a few poor Jews. I saw them being buried. The Jewish women raised a mighty lament, and the cries lingered in the air.

Ten, twelve died every day.

The rain falls obliquely and envelopes the town, and through the rain flow the homecomers.

The newspapers blaze out the dreadful news, and every day Neuner's workers march before the hotel and shout.

XXVII

One morning Bloomfield, Bondy, the chauffeur and Christopher Columbus are gone.

There was a letter to me lying in Bloomfield's room. Ignatz brought it. Bloomfield writes:

'My Dear Sir, I thank you for your help, and take the liberty of leaving you an honorarium. You will understand the suddenness of my departure. Should your path ever bring you to America, I trust you will not fail visit me.'

I found the honorarium in a separate envelope. It was a princely one.

Henry Bloomfield's flight was made in complete silence. Headlights dimmed, wheels noiseless, no sound from the horn, Bloomfield fled in the middle of the night before the typhoid, before the revolution. He has made his visit to his father; he will never again return to his old home. He will suppress his yearning, this Henry Bloomfield. There are some obstacles that money cannot remove from one's path.

In the evening the guests assembled once more in the bar, and drank, and talked about Bloomfield's sudden departure.

Ignatz brought a special edition from the next town. There the workers were fighting with the military from the capital.

The police officer tells us that soldiers have been called in urgently by telephone.

* * *

Young Alexander Böhlaug was going to travel to Paris within the next few days. Frau Jetti Kupfer rang immediately. The naked girls were to take the floor.

At that moment there was a sudden noise.

Two or three bottles came hurtling down from the buffet.

We heard the tinkling of shattering window panes.

The police officer ran out. Frau Jetti Kupfer bolted the door.

'Open the door!' shouts Kanner.

'You think we want to perish in here with you?' cries Neuner, and the scars on his cheeks glow as if painted on in crimson.

Neuner pushes Frau Jetti Kupfer aside and opens the door. The porter is lying there bleeding in his armchair.

A few workers are standing in the entrance hall. One of them has thrown a grenade.

Outside there's a great throng of people crowding into the narrow lane and yelling.

Hirsch Fisch came downstairs in his underwear.

'Where's Neuner?' asks the worker who threw the grenade.

'Neuner's at home!' says Ignatz.

He didn't know whether to run to the army doctor or back to the bar to warn Neuner.

'Neuner's at home!' says the worker to the people outside.

'To Neuner! To Neuner!' shouts one of the women.

The lane empties.

The porter is dead. The army doctor says nothing. I never saw him so pale.

All the people from the bar are fleeing. Neuner gets the police officer to escort him.

XXVIII

Morning comes, along with that slanting rain, like all the mornings before. In front of the Hotel Savoy stands a police cordon. Police are barring the narrow lane at both ends.

The crowd stands in the market square throwing stones into the empty lane. The stones are filling the middle of the street. It could be re-paved with them.

The police officer stands with his suede gloves in the entrance. He holds Zwonimir and me back when we try to leave.

Zwonimir pushes him aside. We creep along, hugging the walls so the stones don't hit us. We get past the police cordon and push our way through the crowd.

Zwonimir has lots of friends. They all call out: 'Zwonimir!'

'Friends!' – a man is speaking from a fountain, 'they're waiting for soldiers. They'll be here by evening.'

We go through the town. The town is quiet, the shops are closed. We meet a Jewish funeral procession. The pallbearers run with the body on their shoulders, the women hurry along, lamenting, behind them.

We know we are not going to see the Hotel Savoy again. Zwonimir gives a sly smile: 'Our room hasn't been paid for!'

We go past the tobacconist's – the one where the winners of the little lottery are posted. I remember the ticket I had.

'Yesterday was the draw,' says Zwonimir.

The shop has been shut up tight, in fear, but the results of the draw are fixed to a wall beside the green door. I didn't see my numbers there. Perhaps they were chalked up yesterday, and the rain has washed them off.

We come across Abel Glanz in the Jewish quarter. He hasn't slept at all in the hotel. He has some news:

'Neuner's mansion's in ruins, and Neuner and his family have taken their car and left.'

'Kill him!' shouts Zwonimir.

We come back to the hotel. The crowd won't give way.

'Onwards!' shouts Zwonimir.

A few of the homecomers echo his call.

A man pushes through the throng and stands out in front. Suddenly I see him stretch out his hand; there is a loud report, the police cordon falters, the crowd rolls forward into the lane.

The police officer bellows out a shrill command. A few paltry shots crackle, some men fall, women shriek.

'Hurrah!' shout the homecomers.

'Clear the way!' calls Taddeus Montag the sign-painter. He is tall and lank, and stands half a head above everyone else. It's the first time in his life he's shouted.

They let him out, and others follow him. Many residents from the hotel force their way through the crowd into the market place.

The hotel manager is standing on the square; he's made his way out here unnoticed. He holds both his hands in front of his mouth and calls out, stretching his head painfully up towards the windows of the seventh floor:

'Herr Kalegyropoulos!'

I hear him shout, and wrestle my way through to him. There's so much going on here, but my interest is in Kalegyropoulos.

'Where is Kalegyropoulos?'

'He's not coming out!' cries the manager. 'He just refuses!'

At this moment the skylight window opens, and Ignatz appears, the old lift-boy. Has his lift really taken him so high up today?

'The hotel's on fire!' cries Ignatz.

'Come down, come down!' calls the manager.

Then a glaring tongue of flame shoots out from the skylight, and Ignatz's head disappears.

'We've got to save him,' says the manager.

A yellow cone of flame darts out like a wild beast.

On the sixth floor the fire is raging, and we can see beams of fire behind the windows.

Now the fifth floor is burning, and the fourth. Every floor is on fire, and now the mob is storming the hotel.

I catch sight of Zwonimir in the turmoil, and call out to him.

The bells of the towers and churches toll heavily into the over-powering noise.

The threatening sound of drum rolls is heard, and the harsh tread of army boots, and a military order bursts out.

XXIX

The soldiers arrive sooner than I'd expected. They stride on, just the same way we once used to march, in broad, capacious double columns with an officer at the head and a drummer to the side of them. In their hands they have their rifles with bayonets fixed, striding through the rain, the mud splashing up, the whole compact mass of men stamping like a machine.

An officer shouts an order and the order scatters the solid, neat ranks; the double rows dissolve, the soldiers stand there like a sparse forest, widely separated from each other, on the Ringplatz.

They ring round the entire block. The mob is now shut up in the hotel and hemmed into the narrow lane.

I never saw Zwonimir again.

XXX

I waited the whole night for Zwonimir.

There were many people dead. Perhaps Zwonimir was among them? I have written to his old father and said that Zwonimir died while in captivity. What would be the point in telling the old man that the boy met his death on the way back to him?

Death came to many homecomers in the Hotel Savoy. It had been close on their heels for six long years, through war and captivity – once death is on your track, it will be sure to find you.

Half-charred ruins of the hotel loom in the growing grey of dawn. Last night was cool and windy, and fanned the fire. Morning brings grey, oblique rain with it, and puts out the last hidden embers.

I walk to the station with Abel Glanz. The next train is supposed to be leaving in the evening. We sit in the empty waiting-room.

'Do you know, Ignatz was actually Kalegyropoulos? – And Hirsch Fisch also burnt to death in the hotel.'

'A shame,' says Abel Glanz, 'it was a good hotel.'

We travel in a slow train together with southern Slav home-comers.

The homecomers sing. And then Abel Glanz starts off:

'When I get to my uncle, my uncle in New York...'

America, I think to myself – that's what Zwonimir would have said – just 'America!'

Biographical note

Joseph Roth was born in September 1894. Born into a Jewish family, he grew up in a household run by his mother, his father being absent, in East Galicia, in a town near Lemberg. Roth would go on to study at the University of Vienna where he took courses in German Literature and Philosophy. His university career was interrupted by the First World War and, in 1916, he signed up and was posted to the Eastern Front. He was later to be profoundly affected by the collapse of the Habsburg Empire. Later to be based in Vienna and then Berlin, Roth initially forged a career as a journalist. His work for leading German newspapers would take him throughout Europe and he became influential and received a regular income.

In 1922, Roth married Friederike Reichler who was later to be diagnosed as schizophrenic and would live out many years of her life in mental hospitals before eventually falling victim to the abhorrent Nazi eugenic programmes.

Roth began writing novels in 1923, initially serialising them through newspapers. He remains best known for his saga *The Radetzky March* which traces the decline of the Habsburg Empire and was published in 1932. Fleeing Nazi rule in Germany, he settled in Paris through the 1930s and wrote prolifically, producing numerous novels and articles, in spite of the demands of exile, publishing difficulties, increasing penury, depression and alcoholism.

Roth died in May 1939 and is buried in Paris.

Jonathan Katz studied Classics and Oriental Languages at Oxford before pursuing a career in research and teaching. He is former head of the Indian Institute at the Bodleian Library and was a master at Westminster School for over twenty years, becoming Head of Classics. He now lectures at St. Anne's College, Oxford. He has previously translated works by Goethe and Theodor Storm for Hesperus.

HESPERUS PRESS

Hesperus Press is committed to bringing near what is far –
far both in space and time. Works written by the greatest
authors, and unjustly neglected or simply little known in
the English-speaking world, are made accessible through
new translations and a completely fresh editorial approach.
Through these classic works, the reader is introduced to
the greatest writers from all times and all cultures.

For more information on Hesperus Press, please visit our
website: **www.hesperuspress.com**

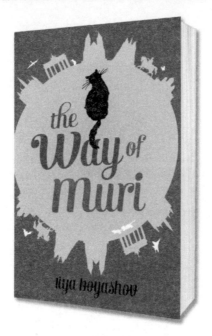

SELECTED TITLES FROM HESPERUS PRESS

Author	Title	Foreword writer
Pietro Aretino	*The School of Whoredom*	Paul Bailey
Pietro Aretino	*The Secret Life of Nuns*	
Jane Austen	*Lesley Castle*	Zoë Heller
Jane Austen	*Love and Friendship*	Fay Weldon
Honoré de Balzac	*Colonel Chabert*	A.N. Wilson
Charles Baudelaire	*On Wine and Hashish*	Margaret Drabble
Giovanni Boccaccio	*Life of Dante*	A.N. Wilson
Charlotte Brontë	*The Spell*	
Emily Brontë	*Poems of Solitude*	Helen Dunmore
Mikhail Bulgakov	*Fatal Eggs*	Doris Lessing
Mikhail Bulgakov	*The Heart of a Dog*	A.S. Byatt
Giacomo Casanova	*The Duel*	Tim Parks
Miguel de Cervantes	*The Dialogue of the Dogs*	Ben Okri
Geoffrey Chaucer	*The Parliament of Birds*	
Anton Chekhov	*The Story of a Nobody*	Louis de Bernières
Anton Chekhov	*Three Years*	William Fiennes
Wilkie Collins	*The Frozen Deep*	
Joseph Conrad	*Heart of Darkness*	A.N. Wilson
Joseph Conrad	*The Return*	Colm Tóibín
Gabriele D'Annunzio	*The Book of the Virgins*	Tim Parks
Dante Alighieri	*The Divine Comedy: Inferno*	
Dante Alighieri	*New Life*	Louis de Bernières
Daniel Defoe	*The King of Pirates*	Peter Ackroyd
Marquis de Sade	*Incest*	Janet Street-Porter
Charles Dickens	*The Haunted House*	Peter Ackroyd
Charles Dickens	*A House to Let*	
Fyodor Dostoevsky	The Double	Jeremy Dyson
Fyodor Dostoevsky	Poor People	Charlotte Hobson
Alexandre Dumas	*One Thousand and One Ghosts*	

Luigi Pirandello	*Loveless Love*	
Edgar Allan Poe	*Eureka*	Sir Patrick Moore
Alexander Pope	*The Rape of the Lock and A Key to the Lock*	Peter Ackroyd
Antoine-François Prévost	*Manon Lescaut*	Germaine Greer
Marcel Proust	*Pleasures and Days*	A.N. Wilson
Alexander Pushkin	*Dubrovsky*	Patrick Neate
Alexander Pushkin	*Ruslan and Lyudmila*	Colm Tóibín
François Rabelais	*Pantagruel*	Paul Bailey
François Rabelais	*Gargantua*	Paul Bailey
Christina Rossetti	*Commonplace*	Andrew Motion
George Sand	*The Devil's Pool*	Victoria Glendinning
Jean-Paul Sartre	*The Wall*	Justin Cartwright
Friedrich von Schiller	*The Ghost-seer*	Martin Jarvis
Mary Shelley	*Transformation*	
Percy Bysshe Shelley	*Zastrozzi*	Germaine Greer
Stendhal	*Memoirs of an Egotist*	Doris Lessing
Robert Louis Stevenson	*Dr Jekyll and Mr Hyde*	Helen Dunmore
Theodor Storm	*The Lake of the Bees*	Alan Sillitoe
Leo Tolstoy	*The Death of Ivan Ilych*	
Leo Tolstoy	*Hadji Murat*	Colm Tóibín
Ivan Turgenev	*Faust*	Simon Callow
Mark Twain	*The Diary of Adam and Eve*	John Updike
Mark Twain	*Tom Sawyer, Detective*	
Oscar Wilde	*The Portrait of Mr W.H.*	Peter Ackroyd
Virginia Woolf	*Carlyle's House and Other Sketches*	Doris Lessing
Virginia Woolf	*Monday or Tuesday*	Scarlett Thomas
Emile Zola	*For a Night of Love*	A.N. Wilson